ISABELLE
the Itch

ISABELLE the Itch

CONSTANCE C. GREENE

Illustrated by Emily A. McCully

A YEARLING BOOK

Published by
Dell Publishing Co., Inc.
1 Dag Hammarskjold Plaza
New York, New York 10017

ISBN: 0-440-44345-8

This edition published by arrangement with The Viking Press, Inc.

Printed in the United States of America

Tenth Dell printing—October 1984
MPC

This book is for all the itches I have known
in the past and, hopefully, will know in the future.
And also for Steffi, who helped

66 "Let's fight at my house today," Isabelle said to Herbie.

"O.K.," Herbie agreed, "but no fair using feet."

Isabelle and Herbie fought every day after school. Sometimes at her house, sometimes at his. They were pretty evenly matched.

Except for Isabelle's feet. She was skinny but she had big feet. She was proud of her feet. She was saving up for Adidas. They were the best track shoes in the world. With those Adidas on, she'd finally come in first in the fifty-yard dash at field day.

Isabelle knelt down on the sidewalk and opened her lunch box. "I knew it," she said glumly, inspecting her sandwich, "sardine and chopped egg again."

"Yuck," Herbie said. "Your mother sure went overboard today."

They inched their way toward school.

"I forgot." Isabelle clapped her hand to her forehead. "I can't fight today. My mother's taking me to the doctor's for a checkup. She wants to ask him what makes me so itchy. She says she might have a nervous breakdown if I don't stop being such an itch."

"Maybe he can give you a shot. They give shots for everything these days," Herbie said, adding another stick of gum to the already considerable wad in his mouth. When it reached the proper size and color, he planned to take it out and stick it on himself, pretending it was a giant boil. Sometimes he stuck it on his neck or the back of his hand or even his forehead.

The boil fooled people. Especially from a distance. Herbie had written to a lot of companies, offering them first chance at his phony boil idea.

So far, he'd had no answers. Once the idea caught on, though, Herbie figured he'd make a mint.

"My mother says she's glad you're not her child," Herbie said, with his cheeks bulging, like a squirrel bringing home nuts.

"And I'm glad she's not my mother," Isabelle said, frowning. "She worries too much. My mother doesn't worry as much as yours does." She stuck her fingers in her mouth and whistled the way her brother Philip had taught her.

A little old lady walking her toy poodle gave a tiny scream and put her hands over her ears to shut out the piercing sound. Her dog yipped and piddled on the sidewalk.

Isabelle and Herbie watched.

"That's the trouble with them little dogs, they're always going to the bathroom," Herbie observed. He knew perfectly well he should say "those" little dogs but he liked to use bad grammar. It made him feel tougher and also drove his mother up the wall.

"If the doctor don't give you a shot, what'll your mother do?" he asked.

Isabelle shrugged. "She'll have to sweat it out, I guess." She walked with one foot in the gutter, the other on the curb, a wounded veteran of foreign wars.

"Your mother and my mother and Mary Eliza Shook and Chauncey Lapidus and everyone you know." Herbie's voice was muffled by the gum.

"Hey, Mary Eliza Shook is a schnook," Isabelle said, as if she'd just made it up. "That's not bad. Mary Eliza Shook is a schnook."

Herbie started jumping up and down.

"I said that last week and you know it," he hollered. "You heard me say that last week. I said it first."

"Take it easy, Herb. You might choke. Don't get so excited," Isabelle said.

One of the best things about Herbie was that he *did* get so excited.

"O.K." Herbie took his gum out and stuffed it in his pocket. School was in sight and if there was one thing Mrs. Esposito couldn't stand, it was chewing gum in class.

"But I *did* say it last week," Herbie said firmly.

Chauncey Lapidus came running up behind them like a locomotive. A fat locomotive.

"Izzy, Izzy, open the doors, in your flowered under-drawers!" he yelled.

"You have green teeth!" Isabelle shouted.

Chauncey didn't stop.

"I hate him almost more than Mary Eliza Shook," Isabelle said.

But for different reasons.

Mary Eliza Shook sneaked up behind Isabelle at lunch period. "Hello, dear, how are you, dear?" she whispered. Quick as a wink, she got her arm through Isabelle's. The worst thing about Mary Eliza was the way she always wanted to link arms with people. She walked arm in arm down the hall, going to the lavatory, and even in gym. That was the worst—walking arm in arm in a stupid gym suit.

It made Isabelle sick to her stomach, the way Mary Eliza did that.

"Have you met the new girl yet? I understand her father's very rich. He's got *three* cars," Mary Eliza hissed from behind her hand.

"So? So?" Isabelle didn't know about any new girl.

"What're you going to give Sally for a birthday

present?" Mary Eliza held on as Isabelle struggled silently.

"Sally who?" Isabelle stopped squirming. She'd wait until Mary Eliza's guard was down, then she'd take off. If only she had those Adidas on right now!

"Sally Smith, silly! She's having a party this Saturday."

As if Isabelle didn't know who Sally Smith was. Sally was class secretary, due to the fact that she could type on a real typewriter. She played the oboe in the school band. She was art editor of the class paper.

Sally was a leader.

Mary Eliza flashed her braces at Isabelle. Isabelle looked mostly at Mary Eliza's mouth. She hated her so much she couldn't stand to look in her eyes. When she hated a person, she only looked in their mouths.

That's how she knew Chauncey Lapidus had green teeth.

"I'm going hiking with my father Saturday so I can't go to any old party." Isabelle's voice always got loud when she talked to Mary Eliza. She didn't know why. Mary Eliza's ears were perfectly good.

"I don't think Sally was going to invite you anyway. Her mother said she would have nine girls and I know for a fact she asked Marsha and Kate and Patty . . ."

Mary Eliza let go of Isabelle while she ticked names off on her fingers. Isabelle put her hands over her ears and read Mary Eliza's lips. When Mary Eliza's mouth stopped moving, Isabelle put her hands down.

But Mary Eliza wasn't finished yet. "It's a slumber party in Sally's rec room. Her father had the rec room soundproofed so we can make as much noise as we like and stay up all night if we want."

Isabelle had to know.

"What the heck's a rec room?"

Mary Eliza raised her eyebrows. "I thought everybody knew what a rec room was. It's to fool around in, to play records, to play games. If it's soundproof, that's the best," Mary Eliza said firmly. "Too bad she didn't ask you. What's the capital of West Virginia?" Mary Eliza hollered suddenly, grabbing Isabelle's arm again.

This time Isabelle was prepared. She gave her a few jabs with the point of her friendship ring. Hard jabs.

"Just because you got a mole on your stomach, you think you're the big banana!" Mary Eliza shouted, backing off. "What's the capital of West Virginia? I bet you don't know."

"Big cheese, not 'big banana,' moron," Isabelle said scornfully, in a good imitation of her brother Philip.

Mary Eliza pirouetted in place, graceful as a willow tree in a hurricane. She took ballet lessons and practiced a lot, especially where people could see her.

"What states border Montana?" she asked, coming to a halt, not even breathing hard.

"Go soak your head," Isabelle said.

"Izzy, Izzy is a bear, in her flowered underwear!" Chauncey Lapidus chanted as he raced by. When Isabelle had been in the first grade, she'd shown the mole on her stomach to the class at Show-and-Tell time. She'd had on flowered underpants. Chauncey had never forgotten, even though they were in fifth grade now.

In a flash, Mary Eliza had Isabelle by the arm again. "Don't let him bother you, dear," she said.

Herbie rounded the corner, a big ring of orange around his mouth. His mother had a thing about vitamin C and insisted he take a Thermos of orange juice to school every day.

Herbie sized up the situation. He was very good at sizing up situations.

"There's a big spider on your neck, Mary Eliza!" he yelled.

Mary Eliza shrieked and let go.

Head up, arms tucked in close to her side, Isabelle sprinted down the corridor, free as a bird. That Herbie was a real pal.

After lunch period, Mrs. Esposito said, "Class, we have a new member, all the way from Utah. Her name is Jane Malone."

All heads turned toward the desk near the window where the new girl sat staring at her desk top. Her sand-colored hair hung about her face in a welcome curtain, her long skinny legs wrapped around the legs of her chair. She looked as if she'd like to be someplace else.

Please don't make her stand up, Isabelle begged Mrs. Esposito silently. That'd be too much.

Mrs. Esposito didn't.

"You're sure you can't fight today?" Herbie asked when the bell rang. "Just a little fight?"

"My mother said to come home after school, pronto. You know my mother, Herb."

Isabelle liked going for a checkup. The doctor had all kinds of neat pill samples and you never could tell what might turn up in his wastebasket.

Mary Eliza and the new girl walked home ahead of Isabelle. Arm in arm they went, the new girl held firmly captive.

"Do I need to bring a specimen?" Isabelle asked her mother, who was pacing back and forth in the driveway when she got home.

"I thought you'd forgotten. Let me look at you," her mother said, holding her by the back of her long shiny brown hair.

"I look pretty good, huh? Do I need to bring a specimen, Mom?"

"The nurse didn't say, so I guess not. And, Isabelle, please behave yourself," she said as they got in the car.

On the way to the doctor's office, Isabelle tried out her police car siren noise. She could do it, after a lot of practice, like a ventriloquist, without moving her lips. Her mother kept looking anxiously in the rearview mirror, driving slower and slower until she was practically crawling.

"I keep hearing a police car," she said, "but they couldn't be after me, I'm only doing thirty."

Isabelle smiled to herself. "You better step on it, Mom," she said. They parked the car around the corner from the doctor's office. "We got a new girl today," Isabelle said. "She's from Utah and her father has three cars."

"I hope you'll be nice to her," Isabelle's mother said. "It's tough being new in school."

"I don't know if I like her. She looks funny and she carries a pocketbook. Of all the dumb things!"

"Isabelle, why don't you, just for once, try being nice to someone because it might make that person feel better? All you think about is yourself. You drive me bananas. And slow down." Her mother tugged at Isabelle, breathing hard.

"You oughta give up smoking, Mom," Isabelle said, taking tiny, slow, mincing steps, dragging behind her mother.

"Try being kind. It would be a new sensation and you might even like it." Her mother pushed the doctor's buzzer. "Snap it up!" she commanded.

"You just told me to slow down," Isabelle said. "One minute you tell me to slow down and when I do, you tell me to snap it up. I can't keep up with you, Mom."

"Well, hello there," said Miss Puffer, the doctor's nurse. Miss Puffer was big and hearty. She hated children. She pretended she liked them but Isabelle knew better. Miss Puffer *watched* all the time. Isabelle had just started to collect cigarette butts from the ash trays in the waiting room when old Puffer snatched them away.

"Mustn't touch," she said coyly, showing her teeth in a playful smile. Isabelle stared hard at Miss Puffer's bottom, which was the biggest one she'd ever seen. Miss Puffer was solid as a rock. Only under her chin where her neck went down into her uniform was she quivery-fat like Santa Claus's stomach. Isabelle suspected old Puffer practiced saying "Ho Ho Ho" so kids who came for checkups would think she was jolly.

The doctor thumped and tapped and poked Isabelle. Finally, he told her mother, "She's in good shape." He inspected her feet and felt her bones.

"She's going to be very tall," he said. "Look at her feet."

There was a silence. Everybody looked at Isabelle's feet.

"She has her father's feet," her mother said.

"No, I don't," Isabelle contradicted. "He has his own. If I had my father's feet, what would *he* walk on?"

Her mother gave her a look calculated to turn Isabelle into jelly.

"Don't be a smart aleck, and don't be so literal," she said. "You know what I mean."

The doctor pressed his fingertips together and stared thoughtfully at them, just the way doctors do on television.

"Anything special bothering you?" he asked.

Isabelle's mother leaned forward in her chair. "One

thing, doctor. She's such an awful itch, always into something, she drives me crazy. I wonder if it's normal. I mean, is there something wrong with her or do you think it's all right for her to be so itchy? It doesn't seem natural." Isabelle's mother smiled hopefully at the doctor.

Isabelle put the doctor's stethoscope around her neck.

"Let's have a listen," she directed, just the way he did.

The doctor unbuttoned his shirt. Isabelle listened.

"Very good, very good indeed," she said, humming under her breath. Blushing, the doctor buttoned up his shirt.

"Don't worry," he said, "she'll get over it. She'll get over it after a while."

"When, doctor?"

Isabelle rummaged through the doctor's wastebasket and fished out a discarded Ace bandage, which she wrapped around her head.

"If I put some ketchup on this, Herbie'll think it's blood," she said, planning. Isabelle spent quite a lot of time planning things.

The doctor looked over the tops of his glasses. Isabelle suspected he wore them to make himself look older so his patients would have more faith in him.

"Perhaps when she reaches maturity," he said. "However, in Isabelle's case, it may take a little longer."

Her mother groaned. "I'll be in the booby hatch long before then," she said. "Put that bandage back this minute. It's full of germs," she told Isabelle.

"That's from my last patient. Fell off his bike and

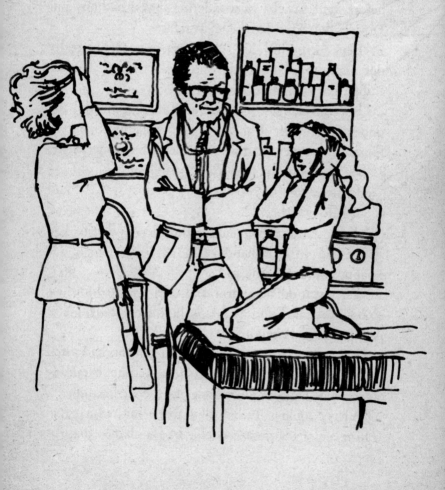

broke his collarbone," the doctor said. "Knit beauti-
fully, if I do say so. Can't do her any harm."

"Doctor, I was reading a story in the paper about
how they give horses pills to make them run faster,"
Isabelle said. "I'm saving up for a pair of track shoes,
but in case I don't have enough money to buy them
before field day, I was wondering if you had any pill
samples that would make *me* run faster."

Isabelle's mother said, "You see, doctor? I'm really
not making anything up. She has a natural flair for
things like that. What should I do?"

"I would suggest a cruise around the world," the
doctor said. "But if that's beyond you, just hang in
there. If you ever channel your ideas and your energy,
Isabelle, who knows what might develop?"

He stood up. "You have my sympathy," he said
to Isabelle's mother.

"Take it easy," he said to Isabelle. "What're you
going to do with the bandage?"

"I've got plans," she said.

"I bet you do," he answered. He opened the door
to his office and said to a lady holding a baby, "You
can bring Fred right in, Mrs. Banks."

Mrs. Banks swept by carrying Fred, who had a red
and haughty face and little squinched-up eyes. He
wore a hat that made him look like the Red Baron.

"That's some ugly baby," Isabelle said in a pene-
trating voice before the doctor had a chance to close

22

his office door. "He looks like an old boxing glove."

Rolling her eyes upward and putting a finger to her lips, Isabelle's mother dragged her out to the lobby.

"Where on earth did you pick that up?" she demanded.

"Dad," Isabelle said. "He said that's what I looked like when I was a baby. And Philip too. He says all babies look like old boxing gloves."

Isabelle's mother hunched her shoulders down into her coat as if she were going out into a blinding snowstorm. Outside, the sun shone with a vengeance that was matched only by the light in Isabelle's brown eyes at the thought of Herbie's face when she rang his bell and he found her, Isabelle, lying on his front porch, bleeding to death from a head wound.

66I went to the doc-
tor's today for a checkup," Isabelle told Philip that
night, punching a circle around him the way she'd
seen boxers do.

"What'd he discover you've got, water on the brain?
Watch your footwork and keep your head down and
your hands up, weirdo. You don't want a cauliflower
ear in addition to everything else, do you?"

Philip showed her how real boxers did it. Since he'd
been in eighth grade, there wasn't much he didn't
know.

"Iz, I've got a proposition for you," he said. Leaning
back in his chair, he tucked his thumbs under his arms.
"You do my paper route for me next week and I'll
pay you a buck."

He made it sound like a lot.

"A measly buck?" Isabelle said. She would've done it for nothing. Next best thing to having her own route was taking over Philip's. "Why can't you do it?"

Philip put on his dark glasses. "Drama Club practice all next week. We have to get our play into professional shape." Philip was president of the Drama Club. He also collected stamps and drew pictures of tall, thin naked people wearing galoshes. At least that's what his drawings looked like to Isabelle. Philip said they could be anything you wanted them to be. "That's the best kind of picture," he said.

"I'll do it if you'll let me ride your bike," Isabelle tried.

"Nothing doing." His ten speed bike was sacred. His parents had given it to him for his thirteenth birthday.

"Will you let me carry the money bag and collect?"

"That'd be too dangerous," Philip said.

"How come?"

"If any muggers found out a little kid like you was carrying money around, they'd mug you and throw you in the gutter."

"Maybe I'd get my picture in the paper then."

"Only if you died," Philip said slowly. "Only if you died."

"I'll do it if you make it a buck fifty," Isabelle said. "I'm saving up for Adidas and they're expensive."

"It's a deal." Philip grabbed her hand and squeezed hard. "Once we shake on a deal, it's like signing a contract," he warned. "You can't back out."

"Please can't I carry the money bag?" Isabelle pleaded. Philip's money bag, which he used to collect at the end of every week, was a beauty. It was bright orange with a drawstring to keep the coins and bills from escaping. They had given it to him at the newspaper office. It was almost the best thing about having a paper route, Isabelle thought.

"I couldn't have that on my conscience," Philip said solemnly.

"If I had my track shoes, I could outrun those muggers," Isabelle said.

"Right. You might even make the Olympics," he agreed.

Isabelle flexed her toes inside her shoes. "They'll probably make me the fastest runner in the world. Faster than the wind, faster than . . . than . . ."

Words failed her. What, after all, was faster than the wind?

"You're a good kid, Isabelle. I knew I could count on you." Philip went back to the crossword puzzle he was working. Isabelle did a little more footwork, keeping her hands up, but he didn't notice so she went to the kitchen and punched around at her mother.

"Cut it out," her mother finally said.

"Maybe I will and maybe I won't," Isabelle said, backing off but still punching.

"Maybe you will and maybe you won't what?" her mother asked.

"Do Philip's paper route for him for a measly buck fifty. He never does anything for me."

"Since when is a buck fifty measly?" her mother wanted to know.

"Can I have a slumber party, Mom?" Isabelle asked.

Her mother shuddered. "Sometime," she said.

"How about tomorrow night?"

"Daddy and I are going out to dinner tomorrow night."

"That'd be O.K. Then you wouldn't complain about all the noise."

Her mother just looked at her.

Isabelle pulled her spelling paper out of her pocket.

"I got a D in spelling today," she announced.

"Not bad," her mother said. "She who is on bottom rung of the ladder can only go up."

"That's what you think," Isabelle said, smiling. "I got an F yesterday."

"You're gaining," her mother said.

Isabelle went upstairs and wrote on her blackboard in big letters:

I HATE MARY ELIZA SHOOK

Then underneath, in small letters she wrote:

i'm gaining

66

"When I get big," Isabelle told her father Saturday morning, "I'm either going to be a tap dancer or a truck driver."

"Aim for the top," he said, kneading his bread. He made bread every Saturday. "Some people play golf for relaxation, some take up needlepoint," he said. "Me, I make bread." Other kids brought Mrs. Esposito a bunch of flowers or an apple. Isabelle brought her a loaf of her father's bread.

Mrs. Esposito was always dieting. She wasn't supposed to eat bread or cake or anything good. But she couldn't resist that bread.

"You shouldn't!" Mrs. Esposito wailed every time, grabbing the loaf before it could get away. "Tell your father he shouldn't tempt me!"

Isabelle practiced her tap dancing as she watched

her father cover the loaves of bread dough with a cloth. She shuffled off to Buffalo quite a few times before she got it right.

"Why do you cover it, Dad?" she asked, fitting a couple of pieces of spare dough around the inside of her friendship ring to make it fit better.

Dancing in time to the music, she sang,

You go home and get your panties,
I'll go home and get my scanties,
And away we'll go,
Oh ho ho, off we're going to shuffle, shuffle off to
    Buffalo.

"It rises better if it's covered," he explained. "Stop jumping around, you might make it fall."

He put the loaves in the clothes dryer, which he said was the best place for letting them rise. Once, when he'd first started to make bread, he'd put the dough in the dryer. Isabelle's mother, not knowing anything was inside, had tossed in a load of clean, wet clothes and turned it on.

That was some nice mess. Isabelle really enjoyed the commotion. For once, it wasn't her fault.

Isabelle took down the bottle of ketchup and shook a lavish portion on her Ace bandage. Her father watched with interest.

"Herbie'll think I've been in an accident," she explained, tying the bandage around her head. "He'll be scared to pieces." She looked in the mirror. "Not bad. We'll probably fight at his house today," she said.

Isabelle's father wiped his hands on his pants, leaving big trails of flour on them. He was a pretty messy cook.

"If Herbie's sufficiently scared, maybe you can win," he said.

Isabelle shuffled off to Buffalo all the way to Herbie's

house. It wasn't easy to be a tap dancer, she decided. Maybe, in the long run, it'd be better to be a truck driver. They got to travel a lot and eat in diners all the time.

Herbie's mother answered the door.

"He went to his cousin's to spend the night. He won't be back until tomorrow," she said.

"He didn't tell me he was going," Isabelle said indignantly.

Herbie's mother gave a little scream. She had just got the full effect of the ketchup. "What on earth happened to you?" She made a grab for Isabelle. "You had better come in and I'll call your mother."

Isabelle darted out of her reach. In a minute, Herbie's mother would have her in bed, a thermometer in her mouth, and would be feeling her pulse.

From a safe distance, Isabelle called, "I'm wounded." She staggered to show how weak she was from loss of blood. A big glob of ketchup oozed out from under the bandage and landed on Isabelle's arm. She scooped it up and put it in her mouth.

Herbie's mother stared at her, speechless.

"It's better when you have a hamburger with it," Isabelle said.

Herbie's mother went inside and shut the door. Isabelle thought she could see her peering out from behind the curtains.

"Goodbye, goodbye," she shouted, racing off in search of some action.

She didn't have far to go. Halfway down the block, Philip caught up with her.

"Hey, I want to take you around on my route now," he said, slamming on his brakes and kicking up a flurry of dust. "So's you'll know what to do Monday."

"What's to know? All I need is a list of your customers and where they live," Isabelle said.

"It's not that simple," Philip said, frowning. "A lot of people think all a paper boy does is throw the paper at the house and leave. People want their paper put a certain place. Some of them are very particular. A lot of them are crabs. You gotta use psychology. Just don't think it's a cinch, because it isn't."

He took out his route book. "We start on Red Barn Lane with Mrs. Stern," he said. "She gives you cookies and she paints."

"Like Grandma Moses?" Isabelle asked. "I saw this neat thing on television about her. She was this really old lady and she started to paint cows and chickens and farms and everything and she sold her pictures for a pile of dough and she never even had a lesson," Isabelle marveled. "She's famous."

"Not that kind of paints," Philip said in his most insufferable tone of voice. "She paints her kitchen or her living room when she gets bored or sad. Last week she painted her kitchen red to cheer herself up. And you never know what color her front door is going to be. Last week it was pink. Today maybe it'll be black."

Mrs. Stern's front door, still pink, opened as they approached. A very small lady with wisps of white hair escaping from the bandana she wore on her head came out.

"I started in on the green," she said to Philip, "and now I'm not absolutely sure I like it. Come and see."

"This is my sister Isabelle, Mrs. Stern," Philip said, very formal. "She's doing my paper route for me next week and I'm showing her the ropes."

"I didn't know you had a sister. Very nice to meet you, Isabelle." Mrs. Stern put out her hand. Isabelle stuck out her left hand and immediately realized her mistake. You were supposed to shake with your right. She always got mixed up. Mrs. Stern smiled and shook Isabelle's left hand as if it were the proper one.

"Do you two fight? I had three brothers and we fought as long as there was breath in our bodies. It didn't mean anything. We liked each other fine. There it is. What do you think?" Mrs. Stern had led them to a small room with a lot of books and half-painted walls.

"You have to be careful with green, you know. You don't want to feel as if you're twenty thousand leagues under the sea," she told them. "On the other hand, the illusion of being in a huge meadow with the sun shining isn't to be sneered at."

She put her head to one side and squinted. She reminded Isabelle of a little bird. Her eyes were very light blue and sparkly. Her sneakers had holes in both toes.

"It looks great," Philip said.

"It's pretty nice," Isabelle agreed.

"The good thing about paint is," Mrs. Stern said, leading them into her red kitchen, "if you don't like it the day after, you just do it over. Have one." She passed a plate of brownies. Isabelle took a long time selecting hers.

"I bet you're looking for the one with the most nuts," Mrs. Stern said. "That's what I always did."

"We have to get going," Philip said, chewing. "There's a lot of things I have to explain. She's only ten."

Isabelle pinched him. Ten wasn't a baby.

"Ten is a nice age," Mrs. Stern said. "I wouldn't mind being ten again. Ten or eighteen or maybe even fifty. In retrospect, fifty wasn't bad either. Stop and see me on Monday, Isabelle. I should have the paint job finished by then."

"She has silver eyes," Isabelle said, running alongside Philip's bike. "How old do you think she is? Why didn't you tell me about her? She's special."

"She's old," Philip said positively. "She's a lot older than Mom or Dad or even Grandfather, I think."

"What's 'retrospect' mean?" Isabelle asked.

"Look it up," Philip said, which meant he didn't know either.

"I wish you'd told me about Mrs. Stern," Isabelle said.

Philip shrugged. "I have forty-eight customers," he said. "You can't expect me to fill you in on all of them."

"But she's special," Isabelle insisted.

"In that house there, for instance," he said, ignoring her, "is old Dragon Lady Cudlip. You watch out for her. If you don't put her paper in between the screen door and the front door, she comes screaming out of the house and makes you do it. You know what she gave me last Christmas? One whole nickel, that's what."

Philip paused dramatically. "A paper route teaches you a lot about human nature. It also teaches you how to separate the cheap skates from the rest of the world, I'll tell you."

They turned into Cottage Street. "Mr. Ball, on the corner, he likes his tucked under the mat with just a corner sticking out."

"Why's he want the corner sticking out?" Isabelle asked.

"That way he doesn't have to open his door on cold nights to see if it's there. He knows whether it is or isn't. It's psychology," Philip said, tapping his forehead. "I'm not sure you're up to all this."

Isabelle had been thinking exactly the same thing but she didn't want Philip to know. She frowned and thought of things like Monday's spelling test and pollution and stuff like that to make herself look older. After she finished thinking, she thought she must've aged a lot.

Philip had three more customers on Cottage Street. "Better give Mr. Johnson his paper next. He lost his job a couple of weeks ago and he likes to see the want ads to see if he can find another one."

"How do you know he lost his job?" Isabelle asked.

"He has this kid, four or five I guess she is, her nose is always running and she tells me everything. They ought to put a gag on her, she tells so much."

Isabelle said, "I think I'll wear my hat when I deliver the papers. And you better teach me how to fold them." Philip had this really neat way of folding each paper into a square.

"It took me about a month to learn how to fold

them," Philip said. "I'm not sure you could do it."

"I can try," Isabelle said.

"You want to watch out for the Olsens' dog." Philip pointed to the Olsens' house. "He knows me, but he might think you were a robber or something. He almost bit me the first couple of times, but I fed him an old banana I had in my pocket and we've been friends ever since."

Isabelle shivered. There was more to this paper route stuff than met the eye.

But then Philip winked at her.

"You're teasing! Dogs don't eat bananas. You're only teasing, aren't you?" She punched Philip on the arm with her friendship ring.

"You ever see me tap dance?" she asked. "I might be a tap dancer when I grow up." The expression on Philip's face showed that he wasn't impressed. It took quite a lot to impress him. Isabelle jumped into the air, waved her arms, and crossed her eyes.

"That's how Mary Eliza Shook looks," she said.

"Crazy," he murmured. He checked his list. "I guess that about covers it. Oh, just don't give the paper to the little Carter creep. He waits for me every day, like he thinks it's a big deal to bring the paper in to his mother himself. Half the time he drops it or can't remember where he put it or he leaves it outside and it blows away. What the world needs is more creeps like that one.

"One more thing. Don't forget to count the papers in the bundle when you pick them up at the drop-off box. Some crooks, if they don't have the right number of papers in their bundle, swipe yours so you're short. And when a customer doesn't get his paper, he calls up and hollers."

"What'll I do if I'm short a paper?" Isabelle asked.

"Buy one out of your own money. Or two, however many you're short. I'll pay you back. And use my bag because those papers get pretty heavy." He handed her the bag, which was old and faded and said *"Courier-Express"* on the side in dim letters.

With that bag on her shoulder and her hat on her head, Isabelle knew she'd feel like a king.

"If only I could collect," she said in one last effort.

"Give up." Philip turned the corners of his mouth down.

"I might ask Herbie to help me deliver," Isabelle said.

"If he does, tell him to leave his boil at home," Philip warned. "My customers might complain."

"O.K.," Isabelle said, "I'll tell him."

Philip rode off on his bike and Isabelle headed for the playground. There was usually something going on there Saturday morning.

In the distance, a figure appeared, leaping, twirling, waving its arms. It was Mary Eliza, practicing her ballet for the entire world to see.

"She is disgusting," Isabelle said aloud. "She is about the most disgusting person on this planet."

Saturday was garbage collection day. Luckily an empty can lay on its side. Isabelle crawled into it and put her chin on her knees, waiting for Mary Eliza to go by. It smelled of old orange peels and coffee grounds and other things.

Presently a pair of feet stopped on the pavement

outside Isabelle's hiding place. The toes of the feet pointed daintily in her direction.

"Oh my," Mary Eliza's voice said, "I expect I'll get the lead in *The Nutcracker Suite* my ballet class is putting on and get my picture in the paper."

Point, point. Mary Eliza's feet spun round and round and round. They made Isabelle dizzy.

A face looked inside the garbage can.

"My goodness, what are you doing there?" Mary Eliza asked, amazed. "I thought you were going hiking with your father today."

Isabelle was speechless for the first time in her life.

"Isn't it icky in there?" Mary Eliza wrinkled her nose disdainfully. "Your mother'll have a fit when she finds out you were inside a garbage can."

"How's she going to find out?" Isabelle got her voice back.

"How do I know?" Mary Eliza raised her eyebrows. "Hey," she hissed, looking over her shoulder, "here comes a lady and I think you're in her garbage can. You better get out fast before she finds you."

Isabelle scrambled out. All she could see were some teenagers whose car had stalled.

"I think it's the carburetor," one said, peering inside.

"Nah, it's probably the points," the other one decided.

"Where's the lady?" Isabelle demanded.

In a flash, Mary Eliza had her arm through Isa-belle's.

"I've got to go buy Sally a present," she said. "Either a photograph album or a diary. Come with me to pick it out."

Isabelle plonked her feet firmly on the sidewalk and took a few swipes at Mary Eliza with her friendship ring.

"Ouch!" Mary Eliza let go. "What'd you do that for?" she asked crossly.

"I felt like it," Isabelle said.

"Oh well." Mary Eliza looked at her wristwatch, which she did about a hundred times a day. "I've got to go anyway. My mother said I had to take a rest before the party on account of we're having it in Sally's rec room that's soundproof and we'll probably stay up all night. It's certainly too bad she didn't invite you," she said sweetly. "I guess she didn't have room on account of she invited Jane. The new girl, you know."

"I couldn't go anyway," Isabelle said. "My mother and father are taking me out to dinner and the movies and my brother's coming and we'll probably stop and have a soda after."

"Don't stay up too late," Mary Eliza said. Forming an arch over her head with her arms, she leaped high in the air, made a half turn, and landed on her other foot. "That's a *tour jeté*," she said. "In case you didn't know."

"So?" Isabelle did a few shuffles off to Buffalo. "You know how to tap dance?" she asked.

Mary Eliza's laugh traveled up the scale, then down. She grabbed Isabelle's arm.

"What's the biggest river in the world?" she hollered.

They'd just studied that. Isabelle racked her brains.

"It begins with an 'A,' " she said.

Mary Eliza laughed and laughed. "You don't know," she shouted.

Isabelle stared at her feet. Sometimes she wrote valuable bits of information on her sneakers if she happened to have them on in school. That was another good thing about having big feet. It gave you a lot of space to write on.

Rats. Her sneakers were clean and sparkling. Her mother must've washed them.

"It's the Amazon!" Mary Eliza shouted triumphantly. "That's the biggest river in the world—the Amazon!"

Isabelle turned and walked away.

"Hey!" Mary Eliza called, "you got garbage all over you. Wait'll your mother sees you!"

Then, as Isabelle brushed herself off, Mary Eliza disappeared, twirling, leaping, and turning.

Isabelle stopped at Mrs. Stern's on her way home. She'd been thinking. Purple would be a good color to paint a room. Purple like an Easter egg.

She circled the house, checking the birdbath and bird feeder hanging from a tree. You could find out an awful lot about a person by checking their yard.

Once, twice she knocked at Mrs. Stern's front door. No answer.

"Up here," a faint voice called. "I'm up here. Giving my gutters a good cleaning."

Isabelle looked up, up, what seemed a great distance, and saw a tiny figure on the roof.

"Watch out!" Mrs. Stern hollered as a mass of slimy wet leaves hurtled past. "Whoops! Sorry. Didn't mean to hit you. Be down in a minute."

And she was.

"How nice to see you again so soon," she said.

"If I got to paint a room the color I want"—Isabelle got to the point—"I'd choose purple."

"Purple." Mrs. Stern mulled it over. "I don't know. It might get on the nerves. Still, it would depend."

"Purple," Isabelle said firmly. "Then I'd have a pink rug and yellow curtains."

"Like a rainbow, sort of," Mrs. Stern said.

"More like a basket full of jellybeans," Isabelle noted.

"It's an interesting thought," Mrs. Stern conceded.

"How come you don't get somebody to clean those gutters for you?" Isabelle asked. "That's dangerous. You might fall and break your leg or something."

"Stella does her gutters and anything she does, I can do as well." Mrs. Stern's eyes snapped. "She's not in as good shape as I am, being older, of course, but don't let her hear me say that, she'd have my head."

"Who's Stella?"

"My sister-in-law, my late husband's sister." Mrs. Stern pursed her lips. "Butter wouldn't melt in her mouth. She's seventeen months older than I am, and to hear her tell it, you'd think she was a slip of a girl. Always telling me how the doctor said he never saw a woman of her age in such spectacular physical condition. She calls me regularly, to check how I feel, how my arthritis is. Always gets it in how she just put up twenty quarts of her famous green tomato pickle, transplanted fifty tulip bulbs, and then topped it off with nine holes of golf."

Mrs. Stern's eyes sparkled. "I ask her why she didn't play eighteen, but, then, Stella never did have any sense of humor. That's one of her big problems. That and trying to get ahead of me. Trying to get ahead and stay there. It kills her that she's older than me. The thing of it is, she never forgave me for marrying her brother. She thought no girl in the world was good enough for him. You should've seen her face the day we announced our engagement!"

Mrs. Stern clapped her hands together and laughed at the memory. "How she did carry on! She simmered down after I asked her to be maid of honor, but there's no denying the rivalry between us. I don't like to tempt fate or interfere with the Almighty, but I do ask one thing of Him and that's that He lets Stella go first. I don't think that's too much to ask, do you, considering she's seventeen months older than me?"

"I guess not," Isabelle said. She wasn't sure what Mrs. Stern meant.

"Where do you want Stella to go?" Isabelle asked. She had discovered that often a direct question was best.

"Why, to Heaven, of course. Where else? I'm not having her outlasting me. How about a glass of milk?"

"No thanks." Milk wasn't one of Isabelle's favorite

beverages. "I better get going. My mother said to come home after Philip showed me his route. He's paying me a buck fifty to do it," she said.

"What're you going to do with that much money?"

"Buy track shoes. Then I can beat every kid in school at field day," Isabelle said. "Usually I come in second. When I get my Adidas, I'll come in first."

Mrs. Stern nodded. She understood. "I used to be pretty fast on my feet, too. Now I jog. That reminds me." She started to run in place. Then she took off, through the hall, up and down the stairs and back to the kitchen.

"I usually get it out of the way before breakfast," she explained, "but today it slipped my mind. Keeps me in shape."

"Mrs. Stern, do you know which river is the biggest in the whole world?" Isabelle asked.

"Let me think." Mrs. Stern closed her eyes and thought. "Isn't it the Amazon?" she asked. "I think it is."

"That's what Mary Eliza Shook said," Isabelle said sadly. "I was hoping she was wrong. But the trouble is, she never is. She's always right."

"I know the type," Mrs. Stern said. "Stella in a nutshell."

When she got home, Isabelle stomped out to the kitchen. It was empty so she stomped upstairs. Her mother was looking at herself in the mirror critically.

"They say lines lend character to a face," she said moodily. "If that's true, I must be some character."

"Why can't I have a slumber party tonight?" Isabelle whined.

"Because your father and I are going to a party, that's why."

"So what?" Isabelle sprawled on her mother's bed, messing up the spread. "We could take care of ourselves."

Her mother looked at her. "Some days I'm too old to be a mother and today's one of them."

"Some days you look old and some days you look

young," Isabelle told her. "This is one of your old days."

"Thanks, that makes me feel a lot better." Isabelle's mother got a long dress out of her closet and held it up against herself. "They say if you never throw anything out, eventually it'll come back into fashion," she said. "Wasn't I smart to hang on to this?"

"Who's sitting?" Isabelle grumbled.

Her mother put blue stuff on her eyelids and drew a mouth over her own with a new lipstick. "Mrs. Oliver has a virus so I guess Philip will have to be in charge. We're only going a couple of blocks away and I'll leave the number."

Isabelle hurled herself on the floor and kicked at the rug. "I won't stay with him," she stormed. "He's a big boss when he's in charge. He bosses me around something terrible. I'll run away."

She stomped into her room and started throwing things around. She threw her favorite copy of the *Wizard of Oz* into a corner, then she opened her closet door and threw her shoes and rubber boots out and started cleaning the closet floor with her shirttail.

"I bet the neighbors would be shocked if they saw the dirt in this house. That closet hasn't been cleaned in a month of Sundays," she said at the top of her voice.

Isabelle's mother was sensitive about her house cleaning. She wasn't too good at it. Nothing drove her crazy quicker than people who said they just didn't know what was the matter, but they couldn't stand a less-than-immaculate house. Isabelle's mother always said there were lots more important things in this world than a kitchen floor you could eat off of.

When she ran out of nasty things to say, Isabelle went to the kitchen and stuck her finger into the jar of peanut butter as far as it would go.

ISABELLE WAS HERE, she wrote in peanut butter on the kitchen cabinet.

Her father stood in the doorway.

"Get a sponge and wipe that off," he directed.

Isabelle scrubbed off the peanut butter while he watched. For good measure, she scrubbed out the kitchen sink. Hard, as hard as she could, she scrubbed until it shone.

Her father inspected her work.

"When you set your mind to it, you can do a first-class job," he told her. He put his hand on the top of her head, something he did only when he was pleased with her. Isabelle stood very still, enjoying the warm weight of it.

"I'll tell you one thing, Isabelle. When you make up your mind to do something, you can do it. Someday you're going to scale mountains," he said softly. "When you stop trying to beat the world single-handed, things will fall into place for you." He hugged her. She smelled the scent of his clothes with delight and thought he was right.

"Mom said I can't have a slumber party," she said.

"Is that one of those affairs where you don't close your eyes all night?" he asked.

Her mother twirled in front of them, showing off her dress and dangly earrings.

"You going someplace?" her father asked.

"The Gwynnes. I told you last week."

"Look how I cleaned the sink for you, Mom," Isabelle said.

"Terrific. It hasn't looked that clean in weeks."

"I don't want to go to the Gwynnes," Isabelle's father said. "They bore me."

"You get to have all the fun." Isabelle went upstairs and looked up Mary Eliza's number.

"Shook residence, Mary Eliza speaking," a voice said.

"Let me speak to Mary Eliza Shook, please," Isabelle said.

Silence. "This *is* Mary Eliza," the voice said in an irritated way.

Isabelle made a very loud, very rude noise into the receiver and hung up.

She went back to the kitchen.

"You have a choice," her mother took two TV dinners out of the freezer. "Salisbury steak or meat loaf."

"You better tell Philip not to hit me," Isabelle said. "The last time you left him in charge, he ate all the ice cream, plus a jar of apple sauce, and he put his feet on the couch. *And* he said I had to go to bed at nine but he stayed up until he heard the car coming."

"How do you know?" her mother asked.

"I spied on him. He called up his friends and swore at them over the telephone too."

"Maybe I better stay home to see that law and order prevails," her father said.

"What if I get a pain in my stomach or a toothache? Philip wouldn't know what to do and I might even die." Isabelle could feel the tears start.

"I'll speak to him before we go," her father said.

Isabelle went to her room and threw a few more things around until she heard Philip come home.

"What do you want?" she said, going down to the kitchen and taking the two TV dinners out of the freezer.

"I'll take the Salisbury steak," he said.

"No you won't. I want it. Mom said I get first choice."

"That's O.K., monster, you made me lose my appetite anyway," he said.

After her parents had left for the party, Isabelle put on her swim mask and flippers and filled the bathtub with water so hot it left a red mark on her as far as it reached. She lay face down in the water looking at the bottom of the bathtub. No man-eating fish there. She kicked as hard as she could, escaping from the mysterious blue whale. When she surfaced, she was gratified to see the amount of water covering the bathroom floor. The ends of her fingers were puckered. She wouldn't have to take another bath for a month, she was so clean.

Isabelle put on her bathrobe and pajamas and ate her Salisbury steak. It was tough. The peas and carrots tasted green and orange. The mashed potatoes didn't taste at all. She threw half the dinner away, then went upstairs to get a sock out of her drawer. Placing it over the telephone receiver to disguise her voice, she made another phone call.

"Hello?" a man's voice answered at Sally Smith's house.

"This is Sgt. Brown down at the police station," Isabelle said through the sock. "We have complaints that you're making too much noise at your house. We might have to send a squad car over if you don't stop all the yelling."

She hung up and made hideous faces at herself in the mirror.

PHILIP IS A FINK, she wrote in huge letters on her blackboard. Wet hair streaming on either side of her face, she lay down on her bed and, before she could stop herself, fell asleep.

$\mathbb{S}$unday morning Isabelle woke with a tickly nose and hurting bones. She was probably coming down with a cold. Her mother would ask her if she was constipated. In front of everybody. Her mother had a thing about being constipated. She dished out laxatives like they were lemon drops.

The sun made patterns on the ceiling. Isabelle lay with her arms behind her head and thought about what her father and the doctor had said. Maybe someday if she channeled her energy she *would* scale mountains. And, when she did, Mrs. Stern might like to go along.

"Isabelle," her mother said sharply, opening her bedroom door, "get out of bed and help me get this water cleaned up."

"What water?" Isabelle asked innocently.

"It's just lucky for you the living room ceiling didn't collapse," her mother said. "What on earth were you doing last night in the bathroom?"

"Taking a bath," Isabelle said, getting up.

"Who was with you, King Kong? The place is a shambles."

Together, using a sponge mop and towels, they cleaned the bathroom.

"What a way to start Sunday," her mother said, wiping her forehead with the back of her hand. "I don't know why you always have to be so naughty, Isabelle. You have a nice home and good food and Daddy and I love you. And Philip loves you."

"He does not!" Isabelle protested.

"In his own way, he does. And you're strong and healthy." Her mother pointed a finger at her. "Think for a minute about children who have to spend days, months even, in the hospital because they have things wrong with them. How would you like that?"

"I wouldn't."

All through breakfast, Isabelle thought about kids who were sick and couldn't do their brother's paper route and stuff like that. Up in her room, she wrote in little letters down in the left hand corner on her blackboard:

i will be good.

She put on her church dress. It was pink with long

sleeves and a bow at the neck. The only socks she could find didn't match. One was knee length, the other an ankle sock. She pulled the short sock up as far as it would go and rolled the knee sock down until it was as fat as a sausage but about the same length as the other. Not bad.

"Let's go!" Isabelle's father bellowed. That meant he was going to church with them. He didn't always. Sometimes he had work to do that he saved for Sunday morning. But when he couldn't think of any work to do and had to go to church, he was always very eager to get everybody organized.

"How come you're going with us today, Dad?" she asked.

"Because he couldn't think of any way out," her mother said.

"Look at Al Blake's lawn," her father marveled. Al Blake lived across the street and had a lawn like green velvet. "He says there's nothing to it, but I suspect he buys sod by the foot and ships it in under cover of night." Isabelle's father had a lot of weeds in his lawn.

Isabelle practiced her police car siren noise on the way to church. She saw her father watching her in the rear-view mirror, so she quit. She knew that he knew what she was doing.

Her mother was much easier to fool.

When they got inside church, their father separated Isabelle and Philip. Years ago, when they were little, they had horsed around a lot, which was why they weren't allowed to sit together. Isabelle still felt like horsing around but Philip was too old.

For a while, she sat quietly. Her nose tickled again. She chewed on a piece of her long hair and put it under her nose to make a mustache. She turned around and twirled her mustache. Some kids giggled. She twirled again. More giggles.

Isabelle's father glared at her. She half closed her eyes and looked at the sun coming through the stained glass windows. The colors ran together and blurred.

The minister said, "Abraham Lincoln said, 'Most folks are about as happy as they make up their minds to be.'" So Isabelle listened. She liked Mr. Lincoln very much.

"If that's true," the minister continued, "being happy shouldn't be as elusive as it seems. One way to happiness is to do things for other people. Try doing a good deed and not telling anyone about it. Try using a gentle word instead of a sharp one. Be nice to someone you don't particularly like. Remember, happiness comes from within."

On the way home, Isabelle's mother turned to look at her.

"That was an unusually good sermon, I thought," she said, giving Isabelle a piercing look. "Did you listen, Isabelle?"

"I like Abraham Lincoln. We studied him last

week," Isabelle said. "Some guy shot him while he was watching a play."

"That was John Wilkes Booth, dummy," Philip said loftily. "Anybody knows that."

"I hope when I get in the eighth grade, I won't be as much of a know-it-all as you are," Isabelle said.

"It was what I was talking about to you the other day," her mother said. "Remember?"

Isabelle rolled down the window. Cold air rushed in. She sneezed. Once, twice, three times. She always sneezed in threes.

"You're getting a cold. Are you constipated?" her mother asked.

"Shut that!" her father yelled.

"Use a gentle word instead of a harsh one," Isabelle said.

Under his breath, Philip sang, "Constipation."

Isabelle stuffed her fingers in her ears. They rode the rest of the way in silence.

Aunt Maude's Volkswagen was pulled up in front of the house when they got home from church. Aunt Maude stopped in every Sunday after church.

"I can only stay a minute," she said, undoing her fur piece. She said that every Sunday.

"Oh, stay for dinner," Isabelle's mother said.

"I wouldn't think of it," Aunt Maude said.

She always stayed.

Aunt Maude was a very little woman who wore very big hats. When she got behind the wheel of her Volkswagen, all you could see was Aunt Maude's hat. If she hadn't worn one, people would probably have thought no one was driving the car. In those hats, she looked like a toadstool. She had tiny feet and wore tiny shoes with very tall heels. Every week Isabelle and Philip bet each other as to whether or not Aunt Maude would make it up the front path, she teetered and tottered so dangerously on those heels.

She always made it, fair weather or foul. She never even sprained her ankle.

"If she falls down and sprains her ankle," Isabelle often said, "we'd have to call an ambulance, I suppose, and maybe even a police car."

"She wouldn't need an ambulance for a sprained ankle," Philip said scornfully. "A sprain's never as good as an actual break."

"Would we have to call an ambulance for a broken leg?" Isabelle asked.

"Maybe," Philip said. "It's hard to say. It would depend on whether it was the femur or the tibia she broke."

Isabelle pondered but did not admit to his superior knowledge.

"How about a police car?" she finally asked. "I thought you called the police when somebody had an accident."

Philip snorted. "Only if she wrapped her car around a telephone pole, and she doesn't drive fast enough for that. The police are too busy to come, except for an emergency," he said, as if he knew.

"I sure would like to have a police car in front of our house," Isabelle said wistfully. "Herbie'd see it and Mary Eliza Shook. It'd drive her crazy. I bet she never had a police car in front of her stinky old house. With the siren going and the red lights flashing and everything. And Chauncey Lapidus. He'd make up a story about how that car was really on its way to his house only it got lost. That Chauncey is some liar."

"Do I smell roast beef?" Aunt Maude asked. "Usually I don't take much in the middle of the day, just an apple and a cup of soup."

Isabelle fixed her brown eyes on her father, but he wouldn't look at her. Last week, after Aunt Maude had left, Isabelle had heard him tell her mother that, for such a small person, Aunt Maude certainly put away a lot of food.

Isabelle went upstairs and put her hat on. Aunt Maude always wore her hat at the table and Isabelle thought that was sort of neat. Just like in a restaurant. Isabelle's hat was red and it had a ripply brim which she pulled down over her eyes. She'd fished it out of the lost-and-found at school and no one had ever claimed it.

Everybody watched her father carve the roast beef. He hated to carve, but he said he wouldn't feel like a man if he let her mother carve. So every Sunday he breathed heavily and muttered to himself while he carved.

Isabelle passed the rolls. She was hungry.

"May I ask what you're doing?" her mother asked.

"I'm passing the rolls," Isabelle said.

"The hat. Take it off."

"Why?" Isabelle asked. "Aunt Maude always wears hers."

"Either remove it or yourself," her father said.

Isabelle sat on her hat. How come it's all right if Aunt Maude wears her hat at the table and I can't, she asked silently. She'd have to check this later.

"That's a lovely cut of beef," Aunt Maude said. "I imagine it cost a fortune." She was very interested in what things cost.

"Well, it wasn't cheap," Isabelle's mother said. "Stop fingering the silverware," she directed Isabelle, and, "Philip, put your napkin in your lap."

Sometimes her mother reminded Isabelle of a general, she gave so many orders.

Aunt Maude's fur piece lay on a chair in the living room and looked at Isabelle throughout the meal. It reminded her of Mary Eliza Shook. It had a nasty little face and a pointy chin. Isabelle felt as if Mary Eliza were looking at her all during dinner. She started making faces at the fur piece.

"Knock it off, Isabelle," her father said. "Another little sliver?" he asked Aunt Maude.

"Just a very small piece," Aunt Maude passed her plate.

"A growing girl like you needs nourishment," he said, giving her a lovely thick slice with no fat on it that Isabelle had been planning on for herself. She hated fat.

64

"I saw your friend Mary Eliza Shook in the five-and-ten yesterday," Isabelle's mother said. "She has such lovely manners. She was on her way to ballet lessons. She practices every day, she told me. Imagine!"

Isabelle crossed her eyes. "Mary Eliza Shook is a terrible loser," she said. "When we play baseball and she strikes out, she throws the bat at people."

Aunt Maude held up a finger. "Not on Sunday," she said. "On Sunday we must be full of Christian charity."

"Another piece, Maude?" Isabelle's father asked.

"Just a tiny one," she said.

Watching Aunt Maude eat, Isabelle thought that Christian charity wasn't all she was full of on Sunday.

After dinner was over, Isabelle and Philip cleared the table.

"You just put your feet up and rest," Isabelle's mother said to Aunt Maude, who had a tendency to break things.

When she'd finished her job, Isabelle stood on her head to watch television. She found it more interesting that way.

"Why does the child do that?" Aunt Maude asked. "She makes me feel all queasy in the stomach."

When the spots in front of her eyes became too numerous to count and the roaring in her ears drowned out the sound, Isabelle righted herself and watched Aunt Maude try to stay awake.

It was a battle. Tiny feet in tiny shoes planted firmly, her big hat on her head, Aunt Maude fought off sleep as if it were an enemy.

Slowly, slowly, her head drooped until it hit her chest, blip! Aunt Maude's eyes opened and she looked around to see if anyone had noticed. After a bit, she'd fall off again and start to snore. Not a loud snore, like Isabelle's father's, but a tinkly little snore that barely made the roses on her hat wobble.

Once, Isabelle had invited Herbie over to watch Aunt Maude fall asleep. That was the one time she hadn't. She'd stayed awake and talked.

Herbie had said, "Always making up stories," to Isabelle. He had been disgusted.

The doorbell rang and when Isabelle answered it, there stood Herbie with his father's army hat on. Aunt Maude looked over Isabelle's shoulder.

"My lands," she said, "he looks like just a baby to me. I didn't know they were taking them *that* young."

Herbie scowled. He didn't like being told he looked like a baby. By Aunt Maude or anyone else.

"Come on out and fight," he said. "But no fair using feet."

"On Sunday?" Aunt Maude was shocked. "I don't think that's the proper thing to do on Sunday. When

66

I was a girl, we weren't allowed to as much as play cards on Sunday. And now this!"

"That's a neat hat," Herbie told Aunt Maude.

She was very pleased. "Thank you," she said. "I think people don't take enough interest in hats these days, don't you agree?"

But Herbie was too busy rolling in the dirt with Isabelle to answer. After they'd fought for about half

an hour and Isabelle was winning, Herbie said, "Hey, I hear my mother calling me."

Isabelle stopped banging his head on the ground to listen. "I don't hear her," she said. Herbie skinned out from her clutches and ran away.

Isabelle chased him home but she didn't catch him. He'd had a head start, that was why.

"You're nothing but a whippersnapper," she shouted under his window. Herbie hated to be called a whippersnapper more than anything.

"A big fat whippersnapper!"

After a while, it started to rain and a cold wind came up, so Isabelle gave up and went home. All in all, it hadn't been a bad day.

She would've written HERBIE IS A BIG FAT WHIPPERSNAPPER on her blackboard, but she didn't know how to spell whippersnapper. So she settled for HERBIE IS A FINK TOO.

"Did you call up on Saturday and make a loud noise over the telephone?" Mary Eliza demanded Monday morning.

Toe, heel, toe, tap, shuffle.

"Not me," Isabelle said. "It was probably Chauncey."

"Did we ever have a good time at Sally's! It was the best!" Mary Eliza rolled her eyes and rubbed her stomach. "We didn't get to sleep until practically morning."

"So?" Isabelle retorted. "So?"

The new girl walked by, her head turned away from them.

"Hello, there," Mary Eliza said brightly. Jane looked startled, bobbed her head in greeting and scuttled past.

"She's very timid," Mary Eliza said. "She wouldn't even go to Sally's party. If you ask me, she was afraid."

"Who did? Ask you, that is?" Isabelle said.

"Listen, dear," Mary Eliza made a swipe at Isabelle, trying for her arm, "I think I should tell you. I think it's only fair."

Punch, punch. Isabelle got in a few good ones on Mary Eliza's shoulder.

"You got the lowest mark in the spelling test," Mary Eliza yelled. "I just happened to be passing Mrs. Esposito's desk and I just happened to see your paper."

"You just happen to be the biggest pain in the neck I ever knew in my whole entire life!" Isabelle shouted. "I never want to speak to you again."

"Don't. See if I care," Mary Eliza said.

"You go home and get your scanties," Isabelle sang, dancing.

Mary Eliza leaped and twirled, a smile on her face in case a photographer were around.

Isabelle stuck out her foot to make Mary Eliza go splat. But Mary Eliza nimbly avoided the foot and came to rest in a pose that made her look like a sea gull landing on a beach.

"That's an arabesque," she explained.

"Who can't do an arabesque?" Isabelle did one of her own. "That's a cinch. Even old green-toothed Chauncey can do one."

"I see London, I see France, I see Izzy's underpants."

Chauncey appeared as if on cue.

"Guess who got the lowest mark in the spelling test?" Mary Eliza asked. "Mrs. Esposito wants to see her."

Stiff-legged, Isabelle stomped in to see Mrs. Esposito. Mary Eliza pasted to her side, trying to link arms. Chauncey brought up the rear.

The only person in the room besides Mrs. Esposito was the new girl, Jane, working very industriously at something, her head bent down so that her chin almost touched her desk.

"My father's making cheese bread Saturday," Isabelle said. "You want me to bring you some?"

Mrs. Esposito gazed at the ceiling.

"Isabelle, how can you do this to me? I gain three pounds every time I eat his marvelous bread."

"You want me not to bring you some?"

"I didn't say that," Mrs. Esposito said hastily. "How about half a loaf? Do you think he'd cut a loaf in half for me?"

"Sure. Half a loaf's better'n none, I guess."

"Listen, Isabelle," Mrs. Esposito said, "I want you to stay after school. I have a list of the words you misspelled on the test and I think it would help if you wrote them out ten times each."

"I have to do my brother's paper route this afternoon," Isabelle protested. "He's paying me to do it and I might even have to collect."

"Liar," Chauncey said. "You're too young to deliver papers. You're only ten. I'm going to call up the paper and tell 'em they're using child labor and they'll probably go to jail. So will you."

"That's enough Chauncey." Mrs. Esposito turned to Isabelle. "You can do much better, Isabelle, if only you'd set your mind to it."

"I promise I'll do the words at home," Isabelle said. "But I have to do Philip's route right after school. Please, Mrs. Esposito?" Isabelle begged.

"All right. If you promise. Everybody get to his seat now," she said as the room filled up.

"Liar, liar," Chauncey said under his breath.

"Old fat green tooth Chauncey," Isabelle whispered, catching him a good one with her friendship ring.

"I think I'm having a slumber party," Mary Eliza said to everyone and no one.

"Order, please," Mrs. Esposito raised her voice.

LIFE ISN'T EASY Isabelle wrote in big letters on her paper. The words popped into her head for no reason.

LIFE ISN'T EASY she wrote again. Every word was spelled perfectly.

You can do much better, she told herself.

66 **I**f you're going to help me deliver, you've gotta take that off," Isabelle said when school was out. She pointed to Herbie's boil, which hung precariously from the end of his nose. "Philip said you couldn't go with me if you had it on."

Reluctantly, Herbie took the lump of chewing gum and put it in the plastic sandwich bag he'd saved from his lunch.

"It stays real nice and clean in there," he explained.

"If you're coming, come on." Isabelle took giant steps.

"I have to let my mother know where I'm going. She has fits if she doesn't know where I am," Herbie said.

"Parents always want to know where you are. Half

the time you're not where you tell 'em you're going to be, so what difference does it make?" Isabelle asked.

"Maybe you're being kidnapped or fell down a well or something and they have to call the police or the fire engines. It makes 'em feel better if they know where you are even if you're not there," Herbie explained.

"How far does this route take you?" Herbie's mother asked suspiciously when they told her about delivering papers. She didn't trust Isabelle.

"Up Blackberry Lane," Isabelle said, making vague motions, indicating the journey, "then around to the left and down. It's a long way," she added. Herbie's mother was about to fire more questions. "I gotta go." She started down the path.

"See you later," Herbie shouted, taking off fast before his mother got a chance to stop him.

When they got to the drop-off box, a bunch of guys with long hair and pimples were standing around, smoking cigarettes and talking in loud voices.

"Looka here," one said when Isabelle opened the box to get Philip's papers. "Whatcha want, kid? Your mama know you're out all by yourself?"

Herbie stood off to one side with his finger in his nose. He always stuck his finger up his nose when he was scared.

"I said, whatcha want, kid?" the guy said again, coming toward them.

"My brother's papers," Isabelle said. "I'm doing his route."

"You gotta be kidding! A pipsqueak like you! Hey, you guys hear the little lady? She's doing her brother's route. How about that!"

The rest of them stood around, spitting and smoking and not doing much else, peering out from behind their hair.

"Where's the fire?" Herbie demanded crossly when they were finally on their way.

"Listen," Isabelle said, "you gotta shape up if you want to come with me. No more finger up your nose. We're going to see Mrs. Stern first and if she sees you like that, she won't ask us in or anything."

"Who's Mrs. Stern?"

"She's really old, only she paints and cleans out her gutters and everything. She has silver eyes, too."

The combination was too much for Herbie. He hid behind Isabelle as she knocked on Mrs. Stern's pink door.

Once, twice, three times, she knocked.

"She's probably deaf," Herbie whispered hoarsely.

"Are you kidding?" Isabelle said scornfully.

"I thought I heard someone, but with the blender going I wasn't sure." Mrs. Stern had on a navy blue T-shirt with CAPE COD written across the front and paint-spattered pants. "Come in and try some carrot juice."

"Yuck," said Herbie. Isabelle stepped on his foot, hard.

"Mrs. Stern, this is my friend Herbie. He's helping

me deliver today. Just for today," she said firmly.

"Hello, Herbie." Mrs. Stern shook hands. Herbie put out his right hand first off.

"It's very good for the eyes," Mrs. Stern said, pouring two small glasses of carrot juice.

Herbie drank his manfully.

"I can see better already," he said when he'd finished.

"How about a refill?" Mrs. Stern asked them.

"No thanks," they both said.

"I've been thinking about the purple room," Mrs. Stern told Isabelle. "It might not be such a bad idea. Or how about a purple front door? That'd be nice and different, don't you think?"

Herbie took the plastic bag with his boil in it out of his pocket. He didn't like being left out of the conversation.

"Do you know what this is?" he asked Mrs. Stern, putting the wad of chewing gum on his arm.

"A wart?" she said. Herbie's face lit up as if he'd just swallowed a neon sign.

"Almost," he said and told her about his idea for making a mint of money.

"I think you might have something there," Mrs. Stern said, passing a plate of cookies. "Definitely."

For a kid with pretty small hands, Herbie sure could palm a lot of cookies in one fell swoop. He loaded his pockets, ignoring the dark looks Isabelle threw his way.

"We've gotta go," she said, making a big deal out of taking only one cookie. "Thanks, Mrs. Stern. See you tomorrow."

Outside, Isabelle said fiercely, "If you don't stop giving me such a hard time, loading up with cookies and all, you can't come again. Where are your manners?" she inquired sternly.

Herbie took a couple of cookies out of his pocket.

"Want one, Iz?" he said.

"Well, O.K. Just one," Isabelle said.

"She's some sharp old lady," Herbie said.

"She jogs too," Isabelle said. She didn't tell about Stella. That was just between her and Mrs. Stern.

At Mr. Johnson's house, the kid with the runny nose was waiting for them.

"Go blow your nose," Isabelle told her.

"I don't got a cold, I'm allergic," the kid said, grabbing the paper.

"You take that right in to your father," Isabelle directed.

"I don't got to, he's at work," the kid said.

Good. Mr. Johnson had found a job. Philip would be pleased.

At the Olsens', Isabelle paused. "There's a ferocious dog here," she told Herbie. "He might give us some trouble but I've got half a sardine sandwich I saved from lunch to give him." She started up the path.

"I'll wait here," Herbie said. He started to put his finger up his nose again.

"Stop that!" Isabelle commanded. He stopped. The dog was shut inside. She could hear him barking. Whew! That was a relief.

There was only one paper left in the bag. Isabelle was tired and Herbie was dragging his feet.

"We have to watch out for the little Carter creep," Isabelle warned. "Philip says he takes the paper and leaves it in the yard, and it blows away and his father calls up our house and complains he didn't get it."

78

The little Carter creep didn't show, so Isabelle put the paper in the mailbox.

"That does it," she said. "Finished."

"I didn't know a paper route was so much work," Herbie said. He took his phony boil out of his pocket. "Is it O.K. if I put it on now?" he asked.

With a nod, Isabelle gave her permission.

Herbie stuck it on his ear. It fell off so he put it on his chin.

"My grandmother came over last week and I had my boil on my neck and she saw it and said my mother had better take me to the doctor right away," Herbie said, obviously pleased. "Even when I took it off and showed her it was only gum, she said boils came from a poor diet and my mother must not be feeding me right. Then my mother got mad and said she did too feed me right and it turned into a big hassle."

They sat down on the curb to rest.

"I'm pooped," Herbie said.

"Yeah." Isabelle thought for a minute. "A paper route does sort of take it out of you, doesn't it?"

"Life isn't easy," Isabelle told Mrs. Stern next day. She held the marshmallows in her cocoa down with the spoon until they got slippery and bobbed to the surface.

"Sometimes it's hard, sometimes easy, sometimes in between. If it was always one or the other, things would be dull, don't you think?" Mrs. Stern replied. "Variety's the thing. Something wrong?"

"I got the lowest mark in the class in a spelling test," Isabelle said.

"Did you mind that?"

"A little."

Isabelle skimmed the marshmallow fluff off the cocoa. "A bunch of kids had a slumber party and they didn't invite me."

Mrs. Stern looked at her without saying anything.

"I minded that more than the spelling test," Isabelle said.

"Of course." The way Mrs. Stern said that made Isabelle feel better. "I remember when I was about your age, a girl down the street from me had a birthday party and invited everybody on the block but me. I thought maybe she'd forgotten and I even went out and bought a present just in case. I can still remember sitting in my window and watching all the guests arrive." Mrs. Stern patted Isabelle's hand. "That sort of thing happens to everybody. Don't feel too bad."

"Can I see upstairs in your house?" Isabelle asked. "I like to see people's houses. Especially closets and attics."

"My closets are always a mess," Mrs. Stern said.

"That's O.K.," Isabelle told her, "ours aren't very clean either."

Mrs. Stern's bedroom was yellow. "Butter yellow or lemon yellow I couldn't decide, as I'm fond of both butter and lemons," Mrs. Stern said. "I made it in between. It's a very pleasant color, yellow is."

Isabelle looked out the window.

"Hey, there's an old lady and a man coming up the walk," she said. Mrs. Stern looked over her shoulder.

"If she could hear what you just called her," Mrs. Stern said delightedly, "she'd explode! That's Stella. And Billy."

As they hurried down to open the door, Mrs. Stern told Isabelle that Stella often dropped in. "She's hoping she'll catch me sick in bed or taking a nap," she said. "Never has yet," and Mrs. Stern knocked on the bannister. "Knock on wood," she said.

"Is Billy Stella's husband?" Isabelle asked.

Mrs. Stern raised her eyebrows.

"Boyfriend," she whispered and opened the door. "Come in, Stella, Billy. Nice to see you. Won't you sit down? You must be tired after your drive."

"You're looking peaked," Stella said before she said hello. "Who's this child?" she asked, her little eyes taking in everything. "You know nothing tires me. Certainly not driving."

"This is Isabelle, my paper boy," Mrs. Stern said.

"I know it's hard to tell the difference in this day and age," Stella said, sniffing, "but she looks like a girl to me."

Billy's shoulders heaved and his nose grew pink. Isabelle thought he was laughing.

"But my dear, of course she's a girl," he said.

"I've got some fresh carrot juice. Good for the eyes. How about a glass?" Mrs. Stern asked them.

"Isn't it strange you should say that?" Stella said. "Only last visit to my doctor, he said he'd seldom seen a woman of my years with such exceptional vision. You look as if you could use a liver shot or two, Ada," Stella said. "Your color's not good."

"Never felt better in my life. Isabelle and I are thinking of painting a room purple. It's her idea," Mrs. Stern gave Isabelle credit. "You don't see too many purple rooms."

"And for a very good reason," Stella shot a dark look in Isabelle's direction. "Purple is a very depressing color, an old lady color. Don't you agree, Billy?"

Isabelle thought Billy had just dropped off for a snooze. He started out of his chair, opened his eyes wide and said, "Absolutely, my dear, absolutely."

"And your arthritis, how is it?" Stella inquired.

"I'm in tiptop condition, never fear. Sure you won't have a glass of carrot juice?"

"We've got to be going along." Stella put on her gloves. "Billy doesn't like to drive on the turnpike so we take all the back roads. It takes rather longer that way but, my, such scenery!" She grasped Mrs. Stern's arm. "Remember," she said, "if you ever need me, I'm there."

Arm in arm, Billy and Stella crept to the car. He got behind the wheel and after considerable maneuvering, pulled out of the driveway and drove off at a snail's pace.

"Old fools," Mrs. Stern said. "Neither one of them can see well enough to drive. She brings Billy along as chauffeur. He's ten years younger than Stella but to look at him, you'd think he was on his last legs. He's a mama's boy, Billy. Always has been, always will be, I don't care if he *was* married for over twenty-five years. His first wife died and left him well fixed. Don't think Stella doesn't appreciate that fact."

Mrs. Stern opened her purse. "I didn't pay Philip last Saturday when he brought you over. Suppose I give you the money for last week and this week and you can see he gets it. I tip him ten cents a week and I'll give you the same." She handed Isabelle eight quarters.

A tip! Isabelle thought the sound of those quarters was sweet as honey.

A face appeared at Mrs. Stern's door, nose pressed against the glass.

"Chauncey Lapidus, you big sneak!" Isabelle said when Mrs. Stern opened the door. "You followed me." Only just in time she remembered her manners. "Mrs. Stern, this is a kid in my class, not exactly my friend."

"Hello, Chauncey," Mrs. Stern said. Chauncey said "Arragh," or something that sounded like it, and tugged at his hair and looked at the ground.

Isabelle stalked down the path, Chauncey a close second. It wasn't until they got to the Olsens' house that Isabelle acknowledged his presence. She could hear the dog barking. Too bad she didn't have a left-over sandwich in her pocket.

"All right." Isabelle turned abruptly, treading on Chauncey's toes. "You want to help, you can deliver here. Make sure you get it under the mat. Tuck it under good so it doesn't blow away."

84

Chauncey's chest swelled visibly. He practically saluted. He took the paper and started up the path. Isabelle saw the Olsens' dog rounding the side of the house.

Even if she'd had her Adidas on, she couldn't have run any faster. Philip must've been teasing about the Olsens' dog, though, because she didn't hear Chauncey crying for help.

That night, after her father had hollered "Go to sleep!" for the third time, Isabelle combined Mrs. Stern's quarters (she'd forgotten to tell Philip about them) with the contents of her piggy bank. She dumped all the money on her bed and ran her fingers through the pile, pretending it was gold and she was a pirate.

Humming softly with pleasure, Isabelle thought that no one at school had ever seen that much money before. What a nice noise it made, jingling and jangling. And what a beautiful bulge it'd make in Philip's money bag! Chauncey's eyes would practically fall out of his head when he saw that much money. And Mary Eliza would have a fit!

And Herbie would flip. Herbie wouldn't be able to fight for a week when he saw all that money.

Isabelle smiled to herself in the dark. (She'd turned out the light because she thought she heard her father coming up the stairs.) The last time she checked Philip's closet to see what was new, she'd seen his money bag hanging on a hook. In the morning, after he'd gone, she'd take it.

"You're going to miss your bus if you don't hurry!" Isabelle's mother stood at the foot of the stairs next morning, as she did every morning, warning Philip. "And if you do miss it, I'm not going to drive you."

Philip thundered down as the bus approached. His timing was superb. He never missed that bus.

Sure enough. The money bag was right where she remembered.

Maybe some other customers would want to pay early, as Mrs. Stern had. And if they did pay her, she'd have to have something to carry the money in,

right? Besides, Philip would never know. She'd be home long before his play rehearsal was over.

When she got out of sight of her house, Isabelle put the bulging money bag in her lunch box and transferred her lunch into her pocket.

"I'm reporting you," Chauncey said when she got to school. "Letting me deliver the paper where there's a monster dog." Chauncey was always threatening to report somebody.

"Where'd he bite you?" Isabelle asked. "Let's see. How many stitches did you have? Did you have to go to the emergency room?"

Isabelle liked the emergency room at the hospital. It was her kind of place, with something always happening.

"It's just lucky for you he *didn't* bite me," Chauncey said.

"It's pretty lucky for the dog too," Isabelle said. "He might've got poisoned and died." She let a dribble of spit ooze out one corner of her mouth to show Chauncey how she felt about him.

"Don't be disgusting," Mary Eliza said.

"Who asked you?" Isabelle oozed a bit more.

"Mrs. Esposito wants you, Herbie." Mary Eliza delivered her message with a smile. She loved delivering messages. "I think she wants to bawl you out."

"I didn't do nothing," Herbie started to stick his finger in his nose until he saw Isabelle frown at him.

The day before Herbie had got a giant splinter in his rear end sliding down an old wooden slide and his mother had rushed him to the doctor's for a tetanus shot.

"That old splinter must've been about a foot long," he told Isabelle. Herbie still wasn't himself.

"Not 'nothing,'" Mary Eliza corrected. "Anything, Herbie, you didn't do anything."

"That's what I said." Herbie put his boil on his neck which was pale gray because his mother let him skip his bath because of the tetanus shot. That boil wouldn't have fooled anyone.

Isabelle took her apple and sandwich out of her pocket. "Where's your lunch box?" Mary Eliza asked. She was the nosiest girl in school.

"It's full of money." Isabelle shook it in Mary Eliza's face and the sweet jingle jangle filled the air. "A five pound box of money."

"You robbed a bank and I'm going to tell!" Mary Eliza shouted.

Nonchalantly, Isabelle crossed one foot in front of the other. "It just so happens it's collection day," she announced. "My paper route you know."

Chauncey made a grab for the lunch box. "I'm going to report you to the authorities if you don't let me help you collect," he said.

"What's all the commotion about?" Mrs. Esposito asked, coming into the hall.

"I like your dress, Mrs. Esposito," Mary Eliza said in sugary tones. She was always complimenting Mrs. Esposito on her dress or her shoes or her pocketbook. She thought she'd get in good and get a better report card if she did that. She made Isabelle sick to her stomach.

"It's a size fourteen," Mrs. Esposito said sadly. "I bought it last week and it's a size fourteen. I thought I'd lost weight but it turned out I was just kidding myself."

They all stood and looked at the ground.

"Mrs. Esposito"—Isabelle handed her the lunch box —"would you keep this for me until after school? It's full of money and I'm scared somebody might pinch it."

"Oh, Isabelle, who would do that?" Mrs. Esposito asked. She carried the lunch box into the room and placed it in a desk drawer.

"Sally Smith's father told her somebody called up Saturday night and complained about noise we were making at the slumber party," Mary Eliza said, narrowing her eyes. "With a soundproof rec room and everything. I bet I know who it was," she said, staring at Isabelle. "I'm having a slumber party this coming Saturday. My mother said I could have all my friends."

"Boy"—Isabelle bobbed and weaved around Mary Eliza—"that'll be some crowd. Both of them?"

"My mother said to tell you she wants you to start delivering the paper," a voice said to Isabelle.

Jane, the new girl, stood with one long leg wrapped around the other, like a stork. She was tall, much taller than Isabelle and her eyes, behind their glasses, were sand-colored to match her hair. She looked as if she were always smelling something bad.

"How'd you know I delivered papers?" Isabelle asked.

"We live on Blackberry Lane. I saw you yesterday with that fat boy. I just happened to be looking out the window and I saw you and him walking by," Jane said.

"That Chauncey. He followed me. He's a pest."

"Anyway, my mother said if you want, you can start delivering today."

"It's really my brother's route," Isabelle told her. "He's paying me to do it this week."

"Well," Jane shrugged, "if you want you can start today. My mother says if we want to be a part of the community we better take the local paper."

"Feel this." Isabelle hefted the money bag. "That's full of money."

"The paper boy we had at home had lots more in his bag," Jane said.

"Does your father have three cars?" Isabelle asked.

"Sure. One for him, one for my mother, and one for my sister. She's a market analyst. My father has his own business. We moved here because he says there's more room for growth here."

"Did you want to move?" Isabelle asked. She'd lived in the same town all her life.

"I hated to. I tried to get them to let me stay with my best friend or even my grandparents but they wouldn't. I cried for eight days straight," Jane announced with somber pride. "My eyes were so swollen I could hardly see."

"Gee," Isabelle said. Against her will, she was impressed. She didn't think she could cry for eight days straight even if she forced herself. "Do you like it now?"

"I hate it. People are snobs here," Jane said flatly. "My mother says nobody even came to call when we moved in. At home, if new people moved into the neighborhood, my mother would take over a cake or a casserole or something. Here they don't even say good morning."

"If your mother helped at field day maybe she'd get to know some people," Isabelle said. "My mother always helps sell hot dogs, puts the mustard and relish on, and sticks straws in the soda. Things like that."

"I don't know," Jane said doubtfully.

"Which house do you live in on Blackberry Lane?" Isabelle asked. "I'll have to buy an extra paper when I pick mine up."

"The white one on the corner of Blackberry and Vine, with the picket fence."

"O.K., tell your mother I'll start delivery today. See you," she said. She'd buy the extra paper at Ken's store. She hadn't seen Ken in a while.

"I see you're in the newspaper game now," Ken said when he saw the *Courier Express* bag on Isabelle's shoulder.

"I just got a new customer," Isabelle said, "so I need another copy. How's tricks with you and Pearl?" Pearl was Ken's ancient hound dog who slept under the counter. Ken called her his watchdog but as Pearl was almost blind and pretty deaf, Ken said he was building up her ego. "Dogs got egos just like humans," he told Isabelle, "and old Pearl was quite a girl in her day."

"We're fine, can't complain," Ken said. "I didn't know you had a route. They're taking them younger and younger these days, eh?"

"It's my brother's. He's paying me a buck fifty and I'm buying track shoes with the money," Isabelle said. "This year I'm coming in first in the fifty-yard dash, anyway."

"Atta girl. I always said that about you, kid, you sure don't let the grass grow under your feet. No sir."

"How about a candy bar for half price, old buddy?" Isabelle boxed around Ken a couple of times and he returned her punches.

"Anybody come in here and see me poking away at a tyke your size would haul me away to the loony bin for sure," Ken said. "They'd get me for child abuse sure as you're born." He reached behind the counter. "Here's a nifty candy bar I been saving for you, kid. It's only half a bar which is why I'm letting it go for half price."

"What happened to the other half?"

"Pearl got it," Ken said with a straight face. "You know Pearl and sweets. She just sorta gums it around nice and easy like."

"Never mind, I'll take a Good 'n Plenty for full price," Isabelle decided. "I better get going. See ya, Ken."

"Not if I see you first," he said.

Mr. Johnson's runny-nosed kid was waiting.

"Whatcha got in there?" she pointed to the money bag.

"Money," Isabelle said.

"Can I have some?"

"Nope." Isabelle handed her the paper. "I'm collecting. Your mother home?"

"She's taking a nap," the kid said. "I got sick last night. I threw up all over my bed and the floor and

95

everything," she said proudly. "I ate something I'm allergic to. I do it all the time."

"Good for you," Isabelle said. "Take it easy." She went on her way, swinging the money bag in wide arcs around her head. When she reached the Carters', their little creep was digging a big hole in the front yard. Isabelle watched while he shoveled the dirt with a measuring cup.

"Whatcha digging, a swimming pool?" she asked.

"Nope," he said, "just a hole."

"When you're finished, what're you going to do with it?"

He thought a minute.

"I'm going to fill it back in," he said finally.

"Cool," Isabelle said. She rang the Carters' bell. Mrs. Carter came to the door. "I'm collecting," Isabelle handed her the paper.

"The boy collects on Saturday," Mrs. Carter said.

"I'm the boy's sister and I'm collecting today," Isabelle said.

Mrs. Carter said, "I don't have change."

"I do," said Isabelle.

"Tell the boy to collect on Saturday," Mrs. Carter said and shut the door.

Oh well. Isabelle shrugged her shoulders philosophically. It wasn't as if she hadn't tried.

No wonder that Carter kid is such a creep. With a mother like that, he doesn't stand a chance.

She rang the bell at the white house with the picket fence and a lady came to the door.

"Jane said you wanted me to start delivering today," Isabelle said.

"Jane, it's your little friend from school," the lady called. "Come in, dear. We're glad of company."

Jane poked her head out from behind a door. "Hey," she said.

"Jane dear, don't you want to ask your little friend to stay and chat?" Jane's mother said.

"I can't. I've gotta finish delivering. I'll see you," Isabelle said, handing Jane the paper. "It's ninety cents a week and Saturday's collection day." Isabelle was halfway down the path before she remembered about field day. "If you want to help spread mustard on hot dogs and stuff at field day," she came back to tell Jane's mother, "maybe you'd make some friends. My mother and a lot of mothers help."

Mrs. Malone looked startled. "When is it?" she asked.

"Next Friday. If it doesn't rain, that is. If it rains, it'll be week after next. And if it rains then, the week after that. They'll tell us at school."

Herbie was sitting on the curb in front of his house, looking dejected. Even his boil looked dejected.

"Hey, Herb, you wanna fight?"

"Nah," Herbie said.

"You wanna do anything?"

"Nah," Herbie said again. Sometimes he got like that.

"I'm having a bad mood," he said.

"You had me fooled. I thought you just won the lottery."

Isabelle went home and watched a soap opera on TV. The lady was either having a nervous breakdown or a baby. Isabelle wasn't sure which.

She dialed Mary Eliza's number.

"Shook residence. Hi, it's Mary Eliza speaking."

Isabelle breathed heavily into the receiver and said nothing.

"Hello, hello," Mary Eliza said.

Isabelle breathed even more heavily.

"I know who it is!" Mary Eliza said shrilly. "I bet it's Isabelle. You better stop or I'll tell my father!"

Isabelle hung up, stomped into her room, and wrote on her blackboard:

HERBIE ISN'T SUCH A HOT SHOT.
I CAN BEAT HIM UP.

What was it Abraham Lincoln had said? Most folks are about as happy as they make up their minds to be.

"Hey, Philip," Isabelle called, "what was the name of that guy who shot Lincoln?"

"John Wilkes Booth, dumb head."

Isabelle erased the blackboard clean.

JOHN WILCS BOOTH STINKS she wrote, and then the chalk broke.

Saturday morning Isabelle woke to the smell of bread baking. It must be late. She got out of bed, pulled up the covers, straightened the spread. The bed looked lumpy, as if she were still in it.

"How's the paper girl?" her father said. The kitchen and everything in it was covered with a fine dusting of flour, like a light snow. Isabelle ate her breakfast standing up, shuffling, tapping. She was getting better at it.

"That's what I like about you, perpetual motion," her mother said. "You'll clean up?" she said doubtfully to Isabelle's father.

"Don't I always? You won't even know I've been here," he said. "I don't think you realize how lucky you are to have a husband who bakes his own bread," he said in a hurt tone of voice.

"I think I do," Isabelle's mother said quietly.

"Today Philip pays me, Mom. Will you take me downtown to buy the track shoes?" Isabelle said. "Field day's next week if it doesn't rain and I've gotta have them for the fifty-yard dash. This year I'm going to win," Isabelle said, loud and sure.

"Is it time for field day again?" her mother asked. "Seems like only yesterday I was dishing up the franks for you and your pals."

"You remember the new girl I told you about in our class? The one from Utah? Well, she lives on Blackberry Lane and her mother said nobody even brought a casserole or anything over when they moved in and I said you'd call her up and tell her about field day so's she can make some friends," Isabelle said in a rush.

"Oh, Isabelle," her mother wailed, "with all I've got to do!"

"You told me to try being kind," Isabelle said primly. "How do you expect me to be kind if you're not?"

"Touché," her father said.

"Where's my money bag?" Philip came hurtling downstairs.

Oh, oh.

"I've got it," Isabelle said. "I forgot to put it back. Anyway, I got a new customer for you and you didn't even say thanks. The Malones on Blackberry Lane want to get the paper."

"You keep your mitts off my stuff or else," Philip threatened.

"Mrs. Stern paid for two weeks," Isabelle said, "so you don't have to collect there today. She said we should split the tip."

"Give you an inch and you take a mile," Philip said sourly. "Next thing you know it'll be your paper route and your customers. Go get the bag, baby."

"He doesn't have to be such a pain," Isabelle said as she marched up to get the bag. "He hired me for cheap and I did a good job, too."

Downstairs again, she told Philip, "I want my money now. I need it."

"This afternoon, freak head. I don't have it now," he said.

"I'll advance it to you," her father said. "So you can get your shoes." He smiled at her. "As a matter of fact, I want to get to the post office before it closes. Let's go right now. Can I trust you to take my bread out when it's done?" he asked Isabelle's mother.

"I'm not sure I can accept such a responsibility," she said. "I'm not sure I'm up to it."

"I think you can handle it," he said. "Tap the crust and if it sounds hollow, it's done."

"Wait'll I write that down," she said and made a big deal about writing the instructions on a piece of paper.

"Your mother is a fine figure of a woman," Isabelle's father said. "A wonderful woman. Just make sure you don't get involved on the telephone and let my bread bake too long."

"Out," Isabelle's mother pointed a finger at them.

"We've gotta go to Newley's Shoe Store, Dad," Isabelle said as they drove. "They've got Adidas there."

"They've got what?" he said.

"The kind of track shoes I want. So I can win the fifty-yard dash."

"What makes you think the shoes make the winner?" he asked.

"They will," she said positively. "They have to. I'm tired of coming in second."

"I hope you're not disappointed," her father said.

"I won't be," she said, smiling.

66"Tell Herbie when he comes over that I went to Mrs. Stern's to show her my new shoes," Isabelle said after lunch. "Tell Herbie I went to his house to show him and he wasn't there. Tell him—"

"Listen, if you have that much to say to Herbie, you'd better stick around and tell him in person," her mother said.

Skimming the ground like a bird, Isabelle took off. She felt as if she wore wings.

"They're beautiful," Mrs. Stern said. "I never saw such a beautiful pair."

"Field day's next week and I'm going to win the fifty-yard dash. That's why I got these shoes. Usually I come in second. I'm tired of coming in second. I want to be first," Isabelle told her.

"I'll keep my fingers crossed," Mrs. Stern said. "I suppose I won't be seeing as much of you now that you're finished doing Philip's route. I'll miss you," she said.

Her telephone rang and when she went to answer it, Isabelle put some sunflower seeds in the bird feeder. Mrs. Stern kept food for the birds even in good weather, when they could find their own. "I like having them come to call," she told Isabelle.

Mrs. Stern came out and sat on the back steps heavily, like a fat woman.

"That was Billy on the phone," she said. "Stella fell and broke her hip. The doctor says he doesn't know if she'll ever walk again."

"I guess she can't tell you what good shape she's in anymore," Isabelle said.

Mrs. Stern's face crumpled up like an old rag. Isabelle was afraid she might cry. "Poor Stella. She'll go all to pieces if she's an invalid. She'll just fall apart. Don't you see?" she asked. "Don't you see that without Stella around to keep me on my toes, I'll wind up being just another old lady creaking around my house waiting to die? It was Stella that kept me going. Mean as she was, she was good for me. She kept me going." Mrs. Stern stared at nothing. "I don't know what I'll do without her."

Isabelle thought about that. She could see Mrs. Stern's point. Sometimes people pushed other people into doing things they might not have done otherwise.

"Mary Eliza Shook keeps me on *my* toes," Isabelle said. "She's plenty mean too. But maybe Stella will get better. Maybe the doctor's wrong," Isabelle tried to cheer Mrs. Stern up. "Doctors are wrong sometimes, you know."

"Maybe." Mrs. Stern didn't sound very hopeful. "You better be on your way now, child. I think I might just have a little rest."

"In the middle of the day?" Isabelle asked, shocked. "You never take a rest in the middle of the day."

"I know," Mrs. Stern said. "But I might today."

That wasn't a good sign, Isabelle thought, as she retied her shoelaces. Mrs. Stern taking a rest. I better go check on her every day and see that she doesn't feel too bad. Then she raced off to the school field to do a couple of laps.

I promise I'll go to see her every day, without fail, Isabelle told herself.

But the days sped by. Isabelle got so involved in preparing for field day that she forgot Mrs. Stern. Her mother called Jane's mother and they made plans for hot dogs and soda. Mrs. Esposito announced that a photographer from the paper would be there to take pictures of the winners. Mary Eliza said she'd probably have her picture in the paper when she got the lead in *The Nutcracker Suite*, so it didn't matter if she won a race or not.

The day of the track meet dawned sunny and warm. Isabelle was up before anyone else in the family. She wanted to have plenty of time to digest her breakfast before the big race.

"Is Jane Malone going to be in the meet?" her mother asked.

Isabelle looked surprised. "Anybody who wants can

be in one," she said. "I don't know. I never asked her."

"It might be a nice idea if you did. There's a good chance they didn't have a field day at the school she went to in Utah. It's probably new and strange to her. I don't know why I didn't think of it before. But then if her mother's going to be involved, she will be too."

"I'm going to stop at Mrs. Stern's on the way to school and ask her if she wants to come watch me race," Isabelle said.

"Oh, Mrs. Stern, the painter. Don't you think that's sort of early to go calling? Especially on an old lady? She probably likes to sleep late," Isabelle's mother said.

"Not Mrs. Stern. She's up with the birds."

Isabelle had forgotten about Stella. She knocked on Mrs. Stern's door but there was no answer. The shades in Mrs. Stern's bedroom were drawn, so she took a sheet of paper from her notebook and wrote in big letters:

COME TO FIELD DAY TODAY AT SCHOOL.
WATCH ISABELLE THE GREAT
WIN THE FIFTY-YARD DASH.

She slipped the note under Mrs. Stern's door and ran off to meet Herbie.

"You're late," Herbie said sourly. "I almost went without you." He hoisted his new pants up under his armpits. "My mother bought 'em big because they shrink when she sticks 'em in the dryer," he explained gloomily.

He stuck his boil in the middle of his forehead.

"You better put that in the plastic bag when you race," Isabelle told him.

The boil slid off Herbie and landed on the sidewalk. He started to pick it up and dust it off. He changed his mind, stamped it flat, and smashed it into the sidewalk.

"What'd you do that for?" Isabelle cried.

"It's no good," he said disconsolately. "It don't fool anyone."

"Sure it does, Herb." Isabelle tried to scrape the boil up, but it was finished.

When she looked up from the spot where it lay, Herbie had already started on his way to school and Mary Eliza, arm in arm with Jane, was walking toward her.

"How come you carry that big dumb pocketbook everywhere?" Isabelle asked Jane, who ducked her head and looked at her pocketbook as if seeing it for the first time.

"Everybody carries one where I come from," she said.

"It looks pretty stupid," Isabelle said.

"Don't mind her, dear," Mary Eliza whispered in a loud voice. "She's not coming to my party. All she does is punch people on the arm. Her problem is she's mean. She thinks she's going to win the fifty-yard dash and get her picture in the paper. Just because she's got new shoes. Let's go," and she pulled Jane with her.

Isabelle crossed her eyes and yelled "Yah, yah," while she jumped in the air and waved her arms.

"Guess who this is?" she hollered. But there was no one to see.

She walked to school alone, slowly, so she wouldn't use up her energy.

Just wait.

"Remember, any- one who has more than two false starts is disqualified," Mr. Brown, the gym teacher, told them. "Wait for the 'go' signal."

Isabelle's heart thundered in her chest. This was the moment she'd been waiting for.

"On your mark, get ready, get set, go!"

A rush of air and Isabelle was off. The wind whistled in her ears, she heard cheers and shouts. It didn't matter. Nothing mattered except that she come in first. She felt free and wild and ran as fast as it was in her power to run.

She crossed the finish line and waited, panting, for the other runners. There was someone beside her, red faced, also panting. Funny Isabelle hadn't seen her up until now. It was Jane.

"I came in first," Isabelle told her.

"Winner of the fifty-yard dash for the fifth grade," Mr. Brown shouted through his megaphone, "is Jane Malone of Mrs. Esposito's room. Second is Isabelle . . ."

The rat, Isabelle thought furiously. She never even said she was going to enter the race. Isabelle felt like taking her new shoes off and throwing them in Jane's face. She stomped off the field and didn't see Mrs. Stern until she called "Oh, Isabelle, I'm so glad I got here in time to see you race. I loved it!"

"Hi, Mrs. Stern," Isabelle said, kicking at the dust. "I didn't come in first. I lost." Her lip trembled.

"What do you care? You ran a beautiful race, fair and square. That's all that matters," Mrs. Stern told her.

Isabelle thought about that. "Maybe," she said doubtfully. "I'm glad you came to see me. Come on over and meet my mother," Isabelle said. "She's the lady sticking the straws in the sodas. Mom, this is my friend, Mrs. Stern," Isabelle introduced them.

"I've heard a good deal about you," Isabelle's mother said. "And this is Mrs. Malone, whose daughter won the fifty-yard dash. She's new in town, Mrs. Stern."

Mrs. Malone was smiling and looked happy. "Isn't it marvelous Jane won? It'll mean so much to her. She's not good at sports as a rule, and it'll be a tremendous boost to her ego to have won. I'm so pleased."

Isabelle left the ladies chatting and walked off by herself. Who cared whether Jane Malone came in first? Only Jane Malone and old Mrs. Malone, that's all. Old sneaky Jane Malone probably carried some kind of magic wand in that stupid dumb pocketbook that helped her win.

"Hey, Iz, the guy's here from the paper and he wants to take your picture," Herbie yelled.

"What's he want my picture for? I came in second."

"He says he wants first and second winners in the fifty-yard dash." Herbie hitched his pants up. "I thought you wanted your picture in the paper."

"Only if I won," Isabelle sulked.

"Shall I tell him you don't want him to take your picture?" Herbie asked.

"No," Isabelle said hastily, "I'll come. Tell him I'll be right there." She rubbed her new shoes on the backs of her jeans to dust them off, then she sauntered back to the field like the biggest winner of the day.

Jane Malone ducked her head and smiled at Isabelle.

That's the first time I ever saw her smile, Isabelle realized. She looks different. She looks happy. So what. What do I care if she's happy? I'm not.

"Will you stop by to see me this afternoon, Isabelle?" Mrs. Stern said.

"Sure," Isabelle said.

"Isn't this the girl who came in first?" Mrs. Stern asked. "Congratulations."

Jane kept on smiling. "Thanks," she said.

"I thought we might get started on mixing the purple paint," Mrs. Stern said. "I've got some red left from the kitchen and a bit of blue from somewhere else and together they make purple. How about it?"

"O.K.," Isabelle said, not looking at Jane. "I'll be there."

"You want to fight at my house or your house today?" Herbie asked.

"I'm going to Mrs. Stern's to paint the purple room."

"Can I come?"

Isabelle lifted one shoulder. "I don't know if she'd let you paint. She might not."

"What do I care?" Herbie stuck out his tongue.

Isabelle went home, stomped upstairs, and took her track shoes off. She put them in the box they'd come in and stuffed them way back in her closet.

She shut the closet door, then opened it and punched the box a couple of times, hard, with her friendship ring. She punched the box the way she punched Mary Eliza Shook.

"I'm going over to Mrs. Stern's, Mom," she said.

"We had a nice talk," her mother said. "Mrs. Stern told me what a good job you'd done delivering papers, how responsible you were and how much pleasure she got from your visits. She told me she thought you were a very dependable child. I must admit at first I didn't know we were talking about you. I thought she had you mixed up with someone else." Her mother smiled. "But it was you, all right. I was very pleased. I guess you're going to grow up after all."

All the way to Mrs. Stern's Isabelle tried to keep feeling sad and mad about losing to Jane Malone but by the time she pounded on Mrs. Stern's door, hollering, "It's me, Isabelle," her heart was light and happy inside her.

"Try a little more of the blue," Mrs. Stern said as they mixed the paint. "And then Stella said, 'The doctor said almost anyone else my age would be bedridden but that, due to my superb condition, I should be up and around in no time.' Isn't that just like her?" Mrs. Stern's silver eyes sparkled with pleasure.

"That Stella's too much," Isabelle agreed happily. "Can we start painting now?"

Aunt Maude stopped in after church on Sunday.

"My stars, when I saw Isabelle's picture in the paper, I went right out and bought ten copies to send to my friends," she said. "And wouldn't you think, buying that many copies, they'd give me a discount? Not at all!"

The feathers on her hat quivered indignantly.

"That's some hat," Isabelle said truthfully.

Aunt Maude turned so they could see all sides of her hat.

"What smells so good?" she said in the middle of her turn.

"Roast lamb," Isabelle's mother said. "Set another place, will you, Isabelle?"

"I wouldn't think of staying," Aunt Maude said firmly. "Are you having mint sauce?"

"And cherry pie for dessert."

Isabelle turned her bright brown gaze on her father. He pretended great interest in something outside.

"It's Herbie," he said as the doorbell rang. "I guess he's come for combat."

Sure enough.

"Come on out and fight," Herbie said. "But no fair using feet."

"Dinner in half an hour," Isabelle's mother said.

"That's the same little boy I saw last week," Aunt Maude said. "Is he still in the army?"

Without speaking, Isabelle and Herbie began to wrestle on the front lawn. Isabelle pinned Herbie down right off and got her knee in the middle of his chest. They struggled silently.

"Oh dear," Aunt Maude sighed and went inside. She hated violence of any kind except in old movies on television.

Herbie looked over Isabelle's shoulder.

"Wow!" he said.

When Isabelle turned to see what was up, Herbie flipped her over and got his knee in the middle of *her* chest.

"You sneak!" she shouted. "You cheated!"

"Say 'uncle'" Herbie said quietly. He was always quiet when he was winning.

"I will not!" Isabelle thrashed around, trying to free herself. "That's stupid. What's 'uncle' supposed to mean anyway?"

"How do I know? It's what you're supposed to say when you give up."

"Who says I give up?" With a giant effort, Isabelle heaved Herbie into the air, using her feet for a slight assist.

"Talk about cheats!" Herbie cried as he hit the dirt. "I said no fair using feet. You lose! You lose!"

"Isabelle, dinner time!"

"I have to go," Isabelle said, dusting herself off. "See you, Herb."

"I'm not so sure." Herbie pulled up his pants. He started for home.

"When I say no fair using feet that's what I mean," he muttered. "She never pays attention to what I say."

66I brought you a present, Herb," Isabelle said next morning on their way to school.

"What's that for?" Herbie asked suspiciously as she showed him the six pennies she'd taken from her bank.

"You'll see. Let's hurry so we're not late." She started off at a fast trot. Herbie hung back. He didn't have to do everything she said to do.

"Say, I saw your picture in the paper," Ken said when they went in. "I showed it to Pearl and she growled. I don't think Pearl's growled like that in five, ten years. I think she knew you."

Isabelle slapped the pennies on the counter. "I'm treating him to a pack of gum," she said grandly, pointing to Herbie. "He can have whatever pack of gum he wants."

Herbie took a long time choosing, despite Isabelle's hissing, "Step on it!" and continual punching and poking at him.

"I'll take the Juicy Fruit," he said at last.

"You don't even have to share it with me," Isabelle said.

Herbie unwrapped a stick. He still couldn't figure it out.

"It's to start a new boil," Isabelle told him. Light broke over Herbie's face. "Gee, thanks," he said.

"I figure if you get a new one started you can sell it and make a mint," Isabelle said.

Herbie put a second stick of gum in his mouth. Already he looked more like himself, cheeks filled out, jaws moving.

"I like you," he said. "I don't care what my mother says."

"My mother said I could have a slumber party," Isabelle walked backwards, facing Herbie. "I'm having Jane and Mary Eliza because she said she might ask me to hers, and Sally Smith."

"Who else?" Herbie stuffed a third stick of gum into his mouth.

"You," Isabelle said.

"Me?" Herbie's voice quavered. He took the gum out and put it in his plastic sandwich bag.

"Yeah," Isabelle said briskly.

"Boys don't go to slumber parties," he managed to say.

"That's because nobody invites 'em. But I figure you're my best friend and I want to invite you."

Herbie started jumping up and down on the sidewalk. "I'm not going to any old slumber party," he shouted. "You can't make me!"

"O.K., if you feel that way about it," Isabelle crossed the street to walk on the other side. "If you don't want to come, it's perfectly all right with me!" she shouted to him.

They skidded into class just before the bell. Isabelle marched up to Mrs. Esposito's desk and put a loaf of bread down.

"Tell your father how much I appreciate his gift, Isabelle, but I've made up my mind," Mrs. Esposito said. "No more bread for me." She stood up. "See this dress?"

"It's nice."

"More than that. It's size twelve. I had it before I got so fat and I dieted all weekend and it fits again. If I ate that bread, it wouldn't fit tomorrow. It's a matter of living with myself. I like myself better this way," she said, smiling at Isabelle.

"That's a gorgeous dress, Mrs. Esposito," Mary Eliza said. "You look super." She handed Isabelle a piece of paper which said:

COME TO SHOOKS HOUSE SAT. FOR EATS
AND TREATS. FROM 7 TO ??????
BRING SLEEPING BAG
AND EAT DINNER BEFORE YOU COME.

"My mother said I should invite you," she said. "Just please don't punch people. I can't stand it when you punch people."

"I don't know if I can come," Isabelle said grandly. "I might be having a slumber party myself."

"Jane is coming and Sally Smith and maybe my cousin," Mary Eliza said.

"I'm asking Jane and Sally Smith too," Isabelle said.

She could feel Herbie's hot breath on her neck. "Maybe I can have mine next week."

"Hello, Isabelle," Jane said, still smiling.

"Hi," Isabelle said.

Sally Smith came in with a note from the principal. "Hi," she said, "how's tricks, Isabelle?"

Chauncey stood on the sidelines, his mouth slightly ajar.

Isabelle did a couple of shuffles off to Buffalo.

"Hi," she said.

All around were friendly faces.

Isabelle took a few jabs at the air, keeping her head down, watching her footwork.

If I channel my energy, I can scale mountains. I'm a dependable child. I like myself better this way, just like Mrs. Esposito says, Isabelle thought.

And it was true.

Tap, heel, toe, tap.

"You know, Mary Eliza," Isabelle stopped dancing, "you keep me going. I don't know what I'd do without you."

Mary Eliza looked stunned. "Well," she said. She didn't know whether to be pleased or not. "Well," she said again. It was the only time Isabelle had ever seen her wordless.

Tap, heel, toe, tap. Isabelle closed her eyes and did a couple more shuffles. When she got home, she was going to take her Adidas out of the closet and put them on. It wasn't their fault she hadn't won the fifty-yard dash. It wasn't anyone's fault. Jane Malone just ran faster, that's all.

"Isabelle," Mrs. Esposito's voice was patient, "please sit down and stop being such an itch."

"Who, me?" Isabelle said.

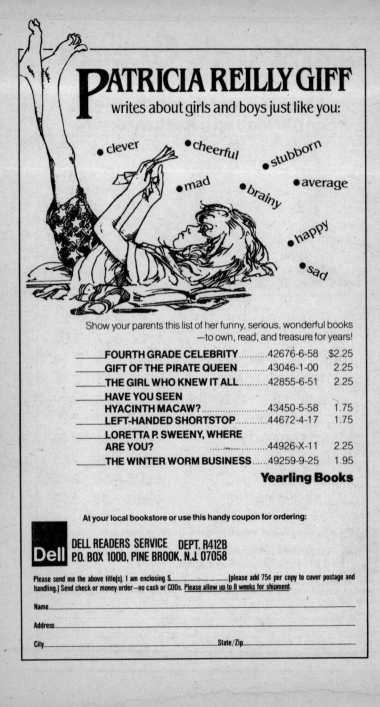